"I'LL HAVE TO REVENGE MYSELF," HE LAUGHED.

Colin was beside her in an instant, lifting her from the chair. Wyeth wriggled, sputtering at him to put her down. Laughing, his mouth swooped, silencing her. She felt herself suspended in his arms, her feet dangling. He tightened his grip on her, and she struggled for short moments, then felt the kiss change. His mouth softened on hers, coaxing her. One hand still held her, but the other came up to tease the tiny hollow behind her ear. She gasped against his mouth, and he moved to take the advantage. . . .

JINX LADY

Hayton Monteith

A CANDLELIGHT ECSTASY ROMANCE™

Published by
Dell Publishing Co., Inc.
1 Dag Hammarskjold Plaza
New York, New York 10017

Dell ® TM 681510, Dell Publishing Co., Inc.

Candlelight Ecstasy Romance™ is a trademark of
Dell Publishing Co., Inc., New York, New York.

ISBN 0-440-14191-5

Printed in the United States of America
First printing—November 1982

To Our Readers:

We have been delighted with your enthusiastic response to Candlelight Ecstasy Romances™, and we thank you for the interest you have shown in this exciting series.

In the upcoming months we will continue to present the distinctive, sensuous love stories you have come to expect only from Ecstasy. We look forward to bringing you many more books from your favorite authors and, also, the very finest work from new authors of contemporary romantic fiction.

As always, we are striving to present the unique, absorbing love stories that you enjoy most—books that are more than ordinary romances.

Your suggestions and comments are always welcome. Please write to us at the address below.

Sincerely,

The Editors
Candlelight Romances
1 Dag Hammarskjold Plaza
New York, N.Y. 10017

CHAPTER ONE

It seemed to Wyeth that she had been driving for hours through the snow-covered countryside. Though the journey from Montreal to Montbel was not much more than eighty miles, the route Wyeth had chosen cut through a rough, almost barren terrain. Ordinarily Wyeth enjoyed long drives, or rather, the free feeling of being on the open road, completely on her own. But the monotonous scenery of this trip seemed to be making the time pass slowly, much more slowly than the last two days she had spent in Montreal, visiting with Monique Almont. Monique had been Wyeth's roommate at UCLA, and though the two women had not seen each for some time, they were still the closest of friends. Yes, Wyeth reflected, the time she had spent with Monique and her family had gone by much too quickly.

The Almonts had been uneasy about Wyeth leaving them to drive alone into the rather isolated area of Quebec, but Wyeth had been eager to drive again, eager to tackle the short trip on her own. She was growing stronger, and she wanted to prove it to herself. She smiled to herself as she recalled the many trips she had taken while at college, then later, when she was in law school. Law school! She frowned for a moment, thinking of all the time she had lost. She wondered if she would need to take her third year over again because of all the class work she had missed while being confined in the hospital, then the long convalescence at home. Did she really want to go back to the grind of law school? Could she take the pressure, the fierce competition?

Wyeth thought back to the long hours of study that would leave her eyes bleary and her mind just a jumble of legal jargon. The eight-hour exams had left her so wrung out that she didn't know where to run first, to the rest room, or to the Student Union for a cold beer. Could she still handle twenty hypotheticals in one quiz? Lord, it had been trying, but so challenging. As much as she had complained then, as torturous as it all seemed now looking back, Wyeth knew deep down inside that she had loved it. She took a deep breath, rounding a slight curve on the almost empty two-lane road. Yes, she would try to go back, to pick up where she had so abruptly left off, maybe even this coming September at the start of the new school year.

For despite this recent period in her life of setbacks, Wyeth knew that she was essentially a very strong-willed person, the type who might be rightfully accused of being stubborn at times. But a person who had always thrived on challenge. Whether it be a course of study or a new relationship, Wyeth knew herself well enough now to admit that she enjoyed pitting her inner strength against a seemingly insurmountable task, or against the strong will of another personality. And wasn't this pleasure she took in rising to a challenge the real reason behind her success in athletics? Wyeth thought so, though others might point to what they called her "natural abilities." Wyeth thought that her success was more likely due to the pleasure she took in striving, to meet most any challenge. Characteristically, she refused to give in, even in the face of impossible odds—a foolish way to behave at times, surely. But then no one could realize how this stubborn will of hers had carried her through the past few months, she reflected, how it buoyed her up when the feelings of bleak, utter desolation had all but overwhelmed her desire to go on living.

As Wyeth eased herself into a more comfortable position in the bucket seat, she lifted the sunglasses from the top of her head down onto her nose. The sky was clear, and the sparkling white fields reflected the strong glare of the winter sun. She was in awe at the depth of the snow. Though she had skied in the Colorado Rockies many times, she had never driven through miles and miles of flatland so deeply buried in snow. She had the feeling she was driving through the Red-Sea parting. Wyeth smiled to herself at her flight of fancy and tuned the French-language station louder, wishing she could understand the words. The houses she occasionally passed were up to their windows in snow and looked like they had been plucked from the French country-side. How could this possibly be ski country? Wyeth mused. Where were the hills? she wondered.

Almost as she thought this, a cloudy hogback seemed to appear on the horizon. Then distant hills marched closer until they were fencing each side of her. The Corvette purred steadily ahead, the hills rising gradually, scattered trees bunching into thickets.

Wyeth took deep breaths, calming herself when she felt the vague stirrings of unease that were familiar. She was determined to be well . . . to be strong.

Larger and larger the hills loomed, becoming mountains of white–pine-dotted beauty. The flat, uncurving road became bendy, dipping in and out of stands of pine and fir. Wyeth sighed, entranced, and drove on.

It wasn't until she had traveled a little over sixty miles that Wyeth would admit to herself that the drive was proving to be too much for her. She could feel perspiration beginning to bead her upper lip, the cold dampness of it making her silk shirt cling to her body. The sleek rental that Mr. Wingate, her husband Judge MacLendon's lawyer, had specially ordered for her drifted to the right as her concentration left her for a moment. Wyeth's wet hands slipped on the wheel as she let the speed drop. She gritted her teeth as she tried to stop the shaking in her arms and legs.

"Just give me the strength . . ."

9

Driving slowly through a hamlet, Wyeth caught sight of a restaurant's flashing sign. Her braking, signaling, and turning were erratic, but she didn't care as she squeezed next to a hunter-green sports car. Even in her dazed state she recognized a Jaguar.

Wyeth shoved her car door open, thumping the door of the Jag.

"Are you always so careless of other people's cars?" a masculine voice grated.

"What? Oh, sorry . . . please . . . excuse me, please."

Wyeth had a hazy awareness of a strong hand gripping her arm.

"Are you ill?"

"No . . . yes . . . please . . . let me by."

Wyeth wrenched past him, putting a quivering hand in front of her as though to ward off the tall, brooding, bearded stranger who was dressed in a down vest much the same color as his car.

Once she was inside the café, she had no idea how she made it down the narrow aisle of booths and seated herself. She took a deep breath as the waitress stopped beside her, pencil poised over pad.

"Tea, please."

The girl who said something in French switched at once to English when she heard Wyeth speak.

"Something to eat, yes?"

"No . . . no . . . just the tea. Could you hurry?"

"There is lovely strawberry *gâteaux*? *Crèmes?*"

"No . . . I . . . I . . . "

Wyeth noticed the tall bearded man standing next to the waitress. Weak and nauseated, she was glad when he spoke.

"Madeline, bring some dry toast and tea for the two of us, *vite, vite . . .*"

Without waiting for Wyeth's invitation or permission he sat down across from Wyeth, his almost hunter-green eyes appraising her.

Wyeth had the hysterical thought that he was the most color-coordinated man she had ever seen—his eyes matching his vest, his vest matching his car . . . his car. Then her eyes slid away from him and fixed on her hands clenched in front of her on the table.

His voice was almost gentle when he spoke.

"You're ill . . ."

"No . . . no . . . after I have the tea . . . I'll be fine . . ."

Wyeth could not remember what else he said to her. She mumbled something to him, her focus on the steaming mug that the waitress placed in front of her.

Sipping greedily, she kept her hands cupped around the mug. The ringing in her ears subsided. She gave a sigh of relief as her stomach stopped doing flip-flops. Her hands steadied a little. She was able to give the man seated across from her a feeble smile.

"Thank you for being so kind. . . . I have to go . . ." Wyeth muttered.

"You're very weak."

"No . . . stronger. I'm fine . . . excuse me . . ."

Wyeth knew she sounded rude, but she didn't want him commiserating with her. The ready tears, never far from the surface when she was very tired, would bubble over and drown the last vestige of her control.

She had to get away . . . on the road . . . reach Montbel. Then she could rest. She would be fine after a good night's sleep.

Her shaking hands left too large a tip as she grasped her bill and pushed herself to her feet. She watched him take the bill from her hand, then she turned away and pushed her way through the door to the outside. She gulped breaths of crisp cold air before getting into the Corvette. She sat there and counted to twenty before switching on the ignition, taking deep breaths all the while. That was something that had always helped her in competition. Just before going off the block in a crucial swim meet or before the first serve in a tying game, Wyeth would use it as her psyche-"upper," her strength-giver. It helped her now.

On the road again Wyeth no longer looked at the scenery. She just concentrated on road signs. She knew she would never have the fortitude to backtrack if she ever missed the turnoff to Montbel.

Finally, after what seemed like hours, her hands cramped from gripping the wheel so tightly, she entered the community of Montbel.

There. There were the mammoth log gates of Château Montbel that Mr. Wingate had spoken of. She had made it.

Relief making her giddy, Wyeth swung the car through the gates and down the narrow, curving crushed-stone drive, touched here and there with the gleam of ice. She released her sweaty grip on the wheel for only an instant and cursed under her breath when the car skidded slowly left, settling in a snow-filled ditch. Wyeth was lightly bumped against the wheel and door, her seat belt holding her fast. She sat there, not moving, her hands welded to the steering wheel.

"You do not have much luck with cars today . . ."

The sardonic smile on the green-vested man stiffened as Wyeth began to scream about the flames, and diving into a blazing pool. Then came the merciful blackness.

Mr. Wingate's voice came from far off even though Wyeth knew she was sitting in his office. She seemed to be floating as she watched both Mr. Wingate and herself converse in his office. Wyeth knew she was in a dream but she didn't mind. She would listen to Mr. Wingate and that other Wyeth sitting in the chair. It was quite comfortable to be a wraith and watch them, even though she knew what they were going to say.

"Wyeth, my dear . . . you look so much better now that all the bandages have been removed . . . and your hair is getting thicker and longer . . ."

With unconscious grace Wyeth put a fragile hand, the skin almost translucent, to the cap of golden curls that hugged her head. Her wide-set blue eyes seemed almost too large in her oval

12

face, the hollows under her cheekbones giving her an ethereal look.

"It is getting thicker. I thought it never would."

Her voice was husky and tremulous when she spoke. Her smile came and went with trembling frequency as she gazed at Horace Wingate. She sat facing him across the kidney-shaped desk that was as pristinely neat and uncluttered as the man himself and his book-lined law office were.

Wyeth's eyes touched restlessly on the thick beige carpeting and the matching beige open-weave drapes. Outside the wide windows behind Mr. Wingate the somber January sky dappled the nearby buildings with browns and grays, seeming to echo the depression she herself was fighting to overcome. How could her husband be dead? The question echoed in her mind. It wasn't possible, she screamed deep down inside of herself.

Mr. Wingate, clearing his throat, startled Wyeth into a semblance of attention.

"My dear Wyeth, as you know, I was not only Judge MacLendon's law partner but his very close friend as well." He paused and cleared his throat again. "After the . . . the accident . . . I mean the first one with your mother and father, I fully applauded the judge's decision to marry you. After all, my dear, you were eleven months in the hospital. You had no one else. Your father and the judge had been classmates at Cornell. They had remained close all the intervening years." He leaned over and patted her hand. "Now, my dear, don't look like that. There is no easy way to discuss this . . ."

Wyeth swallowed, nodding, gripping her hands together as if somehow that gesture would hold her in one piece.

"It's all right, Mr. Wingate. I'm really quite well . . . just this weakness. The doctors tell me it will pass, that I'm getting stronger every day . . ."

Mr. Wingate blew his nose hard with a snow-white linen he had taken from his pocket. He reached for another one of the papers on his desk, lifting his shell-rimmed half-glasses that hung around his neck and placing them in a very precise way on his nose.

"There is the matter of . . . of your estate, after . . . after the second accident—the judge's coronary. God knows, he never even had a warning. Now, don't look like that, child. We wouldn't have wanted him to suffer or be incapacitated. Would we?"

Wyeth's pink-tipped nails dug into her hands, her pallor more pronounced as she shook her head.

Mr. Wingate cleared his throat once more before continuing. "The judge, as your husband, was not only your power of attorney; while you were ill he was also your legal guardian when you were comatose. Even if he were alive that would no longer hold true, since you are, at age twenty-seven, well past the legal age." Mr. Wingate jiggled the glasses on his nose and harumphed once more. "The judge was also the custodian of the estate that came to you from your father and mother. During your long confinement in the hospital and your subsequent convalescence this was excellent. The judge was able to authorize the tests and treatments you so sorely needed, not to mention that very tricky neurosurgical procedure to relieve the pressure at the base of your brain. There were so many times, my dear, when we thought we had lost you."

Wyeth swallowed, remembering how many times she wanted to die, how many times the judge soothed her through her terror when she was blind the first few days, how many times he urged her to live. She struggled against the painful memories that the lawyer's words evoked. She knew with a certain misery that they would soon clog the surface of her mind. Had it only been three years ago that she was struggling in law school? She could remember talking to her roommate, who was also in graduate school at UCLA, but in the Art School. They met as often as their grueling schedules would allow. Wyeth could remember Monique's enthusiastic response as Wyeth had told her that she

14

would be helping her father and mother move east to Boston, where her father had been transferred.

"Wy, it's wonderful. Even if you are staying out here to practice law, you'll still be coming east to visit your folks, and it will be easier for you to visit me in Montreal from Boston than it would be from L.A." Her friend had leaned toward her, a glint of laughter in her eyes. "I told you that you wouldn't have time to swim on a team or play team tennis in grad school. Was I right?"

The shadowy Wyeth in the dream groaned and nodded. "You were right. Just the same, I'm not giving up on either sport. I have never forgotten the feeling I had when I competed in Montreal with the American team. That was the ultimate thrill in swimming for me. Maybe I'll try again someday. Who knows?"

Monique's eyes rolled heavenward. "I don't believe you. Here you are so tall and sexy-looking with those long legs and slim body, and all you talk about are sports."

"Not all. Don't forget Harry." Wyeth had sighed, her delft-blue eyes gleaming as she anticipated her friend's reaction.

Monique shrugged. "How could I forget him! Whenever I'm in his company, he tells me how fruitless it is to pursue a career in art and how I should turn my talents to drafting. If he offers me a job in his father's contracting firm one more time . . ." Monique lifted her fist, her lips pursed.

Wyeth could still hear the phantom Wyeth's protesting laugh as the picture changed again. She didn't want to move away from Monique. She didn't want to see those other images that were moving closer.

Just two weeks later Wyeth had driven east with her parents, she driving her mother's car and following her parents. They had all enjoyed the trip and had taken time to see some of the country. Wyeth only had a month because she was returning to her part-time job, which would keep her in groceries until her last year started in law school. She reveled in the vacation, musing that she hadn't had such free time since the year she had taken to work after her graduation from college.

She liked the apartment her parents had moved into in Boston while the final touches were put to the house they had purchased in the suburbs. She chuckled as her mother unpacked the scrapbook that she kept of all Wyeth's swimming and tennis honors. One framed picture of Wyeth and her parents in Montreal for the Olympics was placed at once on the desk.

She kept in touch with Harry by phone, but though she missed him, she didn't feel lost because her father's friend, Judge Nathaniel MacLendon, was only too glad to talk to her about the law. He had a house on East Avenue, only a few blocks from her parent's apartment. Every chance that she could, Wyeth would walk over to visit with the hearty, distinguished-looking man. Wyeth felt as though she had known him forever and basked in the warmth of his cryptic, intelligent being. He had a gentle but satiric way of viewing the world that delighted her. While her parents would talk endlessly about sporting accomplishments and encourage her that way, Nathaniel would probe her mind, jimmy it into new avenues, letting her see the world in new ways.

One day in the late afternoon, after Wyeth had returned home from visiting Nathaniel, her father suggested that she accompany her mother and himself on a drive out to the new homesite to see the new electrical fixtures that had just been installed.

Wyeth, floating in the background of the dream, gasped with pain as she fought the memories. There was no way to stop them.

"Wyeth, my dear, did you hear what I said to you?" Mr. Wingate had removed his pince-nez and was watching her, compassion etched into the lines of his face.

"What? Oh yes, I understand about the house on East Avenue being deeded to the Landmark Society. Nathaniel explained all that to me, Mr. Wingate, and I concurred with his decision."

"That's good, my dear. I wanted to answer your questions about the other artifacts in the house. As you know, his Rolls-Royce comes to me." Mr. Wingate cleared his throat, tapping his glasses against his cheek in a nervous gesture. "If this doesn't meet with your approval, my dear, I would be more than happy—"

Wyeth raised a hand, bluish veins tingeing through on her fragile wrist. "No, you mustn't think that I would want to change a thing. I want you to have the car that you and Nathaniel fussed over for so many years. In the last two years we were married, through all my convalescence and after, it was very clear to me how much you meant to him and how much your friendship has meant to me. I will always value it."

"Please, my dear, do not talk as though your life is in limbo. You're young and much happiness is ahead of you. I feel that." He coughed. "You're like my own child, my dear, you must know that."

"Thank you." Wyeth whispered, wishing his words had not made the memories mushroom in her mind once more. It was hell to remember.

That warm summer day a powerful car had attempted to pass a roaring tractor-trailer on the upgrade of the country road. Her father's VW, with Wyeth riding behind her mother, never had a prayer. She could still remember the . . . flames . . . the tearing, ripping sound . . . the screaming. Then there was blackness.

She had drifted in and out of the blackness for months. It was a blessed relief from the pain of the burns, her horribly pounding head that had been shaved and swathed in bandages. It took months to move . . . sit up . . . to walk without pain and the aid of crutches. The weight melted from her slim frame.

Through it all Nathaniel's face was there—his shock of white hair like a mane flowing back from his high forehead. He held her tight when he told her that her parents had died instantly. He had held her close through all the pain. She had been glad to put her hand in his and marry him so that all the decisions would be his. His eyes were like green sparks that put life into her. She had been happy to come home to the Victorian mansion to recuperate. She gained strength on the walks she took with

17

Nathaniel as he pointed out the mansions and told her the histories of the families who owned the great houses in Boston. She was getting well. Wyeth could feel it. A cocoon of safety was hers for two years.

One night the housekeeper, Mrs. Boggs, woke her to tell her that the doctor was with Nathaniel. He had had a coronary, but he was expected to recover. He didn't live through the night. Wyeth was alone again. Monique came to stay in the big house on the avenue to help Wyeth in her recovery of yet another operation, cosmetic surgery to graft more skin from her leg to her badly burned back. It had been her third operation in the year since she had lived in the house with Nathaniel. Now he was no longer there to help her through the ordeal.

Again Wyeth's dream faded, taking her back to Mr. Wingate's office. She watched Mr. Wingate's expression as he looked at the other Wyeth still sitting in the same chair.

"You do understand, don't you, my dear? Since you are twenty-seven, you will have complete control of your estate, except for Montbel. That you will share in joint guardianship with the other MacLendons. With the rest of the family and your share it comes to fifty-one percent of the stock. The largest single shareholder is the judge's nephew, Colin MacLendon." Mr. Wingate cleared his throat once more. "I know this might seem a bit complicated to you, but Nathaniel bestowed all his votes on his nephew, Colin, trusting to his business acumen. The trust was not unfounded, since the growth of Montbel into one of the finest resorts in North America, is largely attributable to Colin. He is a very tough, shrewd administrator, though he sometimes comes to cuffs with some of the other members of the family."

"I remember Nathaniel describing him to me but we've never met. He sounded quite ruthless to me, but Nathaniel seemed to like him."

Mr. Wingate gave a rumbly, deep laugh. "Well, yes, I suppose you could describe him as ruthless when he's crossed, but to be just, I think he has had to be. He's quite wealthy apart from

18

Montbel, but he took over the running of it eight years ago when he was just twenty-eight and brought it through a very precarious financial time. Many times I thought he might go under, but he fought it through so that today Montbel is solidly in the black. And that, my dear, is a coup in these inflationary times. Very reliable man. I like him, but, of course . . . ah, well, never mind that." He adjusted his glasses again. "Wyeth, I wish you could see Montbel. Ah, no lovelier place on earth than Montbel, I do believe. The jewel of Quebec, I would say. Mountains for skiing, trails for cross-country skiing, golf courses, tennis courts, rivers, pools. They do say that the seigneury is over a hundred square miles."

Wyeth gasped. "Could that be? Mr. Wingate, I had no idea . . . Nathaniel never said how large it was."

Mr. Wingate studied her in a solemn, owlish way. "Indeed, my dear, some of the holdings in Quebec go back to King Louis. The MacLendon family has been in Quebec since before our Revolution. One of the early members of the family married a wealthy French-Canadian girl, hence the acquisition of the seigneury. By inheritance you are now a partial legal holder of the seigneury. Now, you have told me that you are interested in the cash settlement that Colin MacLendon has offered you through this office. Is that right?" At her nod Mr. Wingate continued. "All right, my dear, I can handle that for you. I suppose it is the right thing to do . . . but I wish that you could see Montbel and then make your decision." He shrugged.

Wyeth looked out the window at the gray January day. "Perhaps it would help to get away. I would like to see the place that Nathaniel loved so much. Maybe I could go up there for a short stay." She faltered.

Mr. Wingate clapped his hands together, jumping to his feet with an energy that belied his years. "Capital, my dear, capital. It would be just the thing for you while you're recuperating. It's too bad I didn't mention something to Colin when he was here for Nathaniel's funeral. He was very understanding about you

19

not seeing anyone but the Almonts and myself in your weakened condition. I didn't think of it then."

Wyeth smiled at the rueful frown on the lawyer's face before it brightened again in a beatific smile that made him look like an aging cherub.

"No matter," he rubbed his hands again, "I'll take care of it now. You deserve to be happy, Wyeth. At twenty-seven your life is all in front of you. Promise me you will try to be happy, if not for my sake, then for Nathaniel's."

Wyeth's eyes filled with tears as she placed a brusque kiss on her cheek and led her from the office down to the waiting taxicab.

Yes, she was still young and had so much of her life before her. She would heal, grow strong again, emotionally and physically. Yet some small nagging voice seemed to whisper a warning at times when Wyeth least expected. Don't get too happy, Wyeth, the voice seemed to say. You weren't meant for that. And Wyeth, being Wyeth, would dismiss the voice, ignore it. With all the heartache she had suffered in the past two years, she had every right to happiness now—every right and *more*, she assured herself. She would travel to Montbel, she decided suddenly; a change of scenery was just what she needed.

All at once Wyeth knew there was much she wanted to say to Mr. Wingate. There were questions that she wanted to ask about Montbel and the faceless Colin MacLendon. She wanted to tell Mr. Wingate that she was getting stronger, that she would be able to handle the unknown Mr. MacLendon. She wanted to tell him that she had every intention of going back and finishing law school as soon as she was able, that somehow she was going to pick up the threads of her life.

The Wyeth lying in the bed called to him to stop the other Wyeth from entering the cab so that she could tell him. Why didn't he hear her?

She watched his hand guide Wyeth into the vehicle; then his hand began melting into the grayness. She called to him to come back.

Wyeth woke, her eyes heavy and reluctant, puzzled that Mrs. Boggs had replaced her bedroom-window sheers with swagged-back linen drapes of old gold-and-cinnamon plaid.

"Well, young lady . . ."

The hearty voice pulled Wyeth's head around. She tried to fix her hazy sight on the heavyset man bending over her.

". . . you have given everyone a scare. I am Dr. Tiant, not your Mr. Wingate. There, there, do not be frightened, *ma fille,* you are at Montbel, and you are safe. Such terror you have lived in your dreams, *enfant* . . . but you are safe now. You understand, yes?"

"Yes, I understand . . . thank you, Doctor—the car—it isn't mine . . ."

"The car is fine, hardly a scratch. It was pulled easily from the ditch with the tractor. The piles of snow cushioned the car and you. Still, I would say that the condition of the car is far better than you, *petite.* I can see from my examination that you are recuperating from grave injuries. Your head . . . hip . . . of course they are mending well—but, what on earth happened to you, *pauvre?*"

Wyeth sketched the accident as rapidly as she could, holding herself in control. She had the feeling that Dr. Tiant was seeing volumes behind every word.

"So . . . my little one, that is why you had such a severe reaction to such a minor incident. What a terrible thing to happen. Your burns and injuries are doing well, as I said, but the weakness will be with you for some time. It was foolish of you to drive any distance. Ah, well, you are here. Were you planning to holiday at Montbel? There is no more beautiful spot anywhere . . ."

Before Wyeth could answer, the door to the suite swung open. The green-vested, bearded man stood there. He had shed his vest, but Wyeth knew him. She had the strange feeling that she would know him even if he were shrouded in a mask and domino. Instead of bal-masqué dress he had a cream-colored turtleneck shirt stretched across his broad shoulders, the color enhancing the copper lights of his deep-brown hair. His long, muscular legs were sheathed in black corded jeans that hugged his narrow hips. Wyeth's eyes were drawn to his. They were like liquid green fire warming her, comforting her.

Wyeth knew she would have to thank this man so that he could be on his way. She swallowed several times, trying to lubricate her dry throat in order to form words. Before she could find the strength, he spoke.

"Well, Émile, have we finished her off?"

"No, Colin, she . . ."

Wyeth didn't hear the rest of what the doctor was saying. She stared harder at the one called Colin. Was this Colin MacLendon? Nathaniel's nephew? No wonder his eyes had soothed her. He had Nathaniel's eyes. His voice penetrated her musings.

"Well, Miss Crane of the California driver's license, how do you feel? It's too bad you didn't mention you were coming to Montbel when we were at Gaspard's. We could have left your car there and come here in mine. Someone could have picked up your car later. Then this . . ." He gave an impatient sweep of his hand toward the bed. ". . . might have been avoided."

"Now, Colin, I won't let you bully my patient . . ."

Dr. Tiant's kind words brought the tears to Wyeth's eyes. They flooded down her cheeks. She felt helpless, unable to control the deluge.

"Now, now, my little one, pay no attention to him. Pretty soon the shot I gave you will take effect, yes? Then you will sleep . . ."

Wyeth kept her eyes on Dr. Tiant, hoping that the one called Colin would go away.

CHAPTER TWO

Wyeth woke again in the gold-and-cinnamon–plaid suite. She focused on the one wall that was logs, the same as the outer siding of the château. Two other walls of the room were painted a pale creamy gold. Through the open door in the log wall she glimpsed couches and chairs and guessed it to be a sitting room. Clear, bright sunlight streamed through sliding glass doors that formed the fourth wall of the suite. These led to a small wooden balcony now covered with snow.

Wyeth heard the click of a key turning and watched the door swing slowly open. She pulled the bedclothes up around her. A plump, smiling young woman stood in the doorway.

"*Bonjour, mademoiselle, je*—"

"Please, pardon me, but I don't speak French . . ."

"Ah, *oui,* well, then I will speak English. I speak good. Here is your breakfast, Miss Crane. The doctor says if you are feeling strong enough, that you may get up after you eat. I am Marie, and I am to help you, *mademoiselle* . . ."

"What time is it, Marie?"

"Eleven o'clock, Miss Crane . . ."

"Good Lord, is it really? By the way, Marie, my name is MacLendon. I am Mrs. Nathaniel MacLendon, Marie. Just put the tray there, please . . ." Wyeth swallowed hard and licked her lips, trying to dispel the cotton-wool taste in her mouth, the aftermath of the sedative Dr. Tiant had given her.

The open-mouthed Marie placed the tray across Wyeth's

knees, holding it firm as Wyeth settled herself against the cushions behind her.

"*Mais*, but, how is this, *mademois—madame*? You are Miss Crane, are you not?"

"Yes, Marie, I was Miss Crane before I married Judge MacLendon. Thank you, yes, I would prefer the coffeepot on the table, please. I'm fine now, thank you."

Marie was reluctant to go. Wyeth could tell by the way she kept turning her head as she went to the door. Wyeth took mischievous delight in not satisfying the young woman's curiosity any further.

The aroma from the heavily laden silver tray and covered dishes made her forget the maid and everything else except her burgeoning hunger. Before the auto accident Wyeth had had a healthy athlete's attitude toward food. She was able to eat quantities of anything and everything and never gain weight. Since the accident and dramatic loss of weight, her appetite had been almost birdlike. Of course, she did not gain the weight that she needed, either.

As she gazed at the fluffy, light-as-a-cloud, mushroom omelet and silver basket of freshly baked croissants, she felt her first mouth-watering pangs of appetite.

The food was luscious, the coffee dark and rich. Still, she couldn't finish all of the meal—half of the omelet and one croissant filled her to bursting. She felt relaxed and appeased.

As she lay there she couldn't help but think of the Almonts and how kind they had been to her when she was in Montreal. Was it only yesterday that she had left that lovely city to drive to Montbel?

She closed her eyes for a moment and savored that meeting with such good friends.

The Almonts had shown her Old Montreal, and she had been enchanted. She had not seen much of the city: the only other time had been seven years ago when she had competed in the Summer Olympics for the United States. The Almonts had taken her to

Gibby's, where she had dined on succulent steaks. Though she had loved the food and had been delighted with the complicated ritual of Irish coffee, it had all been too much for her shrunken appetite. She had relaxed a little and felt comforted by the Almonts and Monique.

"Wyeth, dear, I can't believe that you have rented a car to drive to Montbel. Won't it be too much for you, dear, after . . . well . . . it was a long convalescence, wasn't it?"

Wyeth remembered being warmed by Mrs. Almont's concern but shook her head in the negative. "Don't worry, it won't be too much for me; I want to drive, see something of the countryside. Being in a car doesn't bother me, really . . ."

The older woman had hugged her. "Are you sure, my dear? You were almost a year in the hospital. I hope . . ."

Wyeth smiled to herself as she remembered how Mr. Almont had shushed his wife. Monique had embraced her with a watery smile when they parted.

She opened her eyes, stretching, the memory of her friends comforting her. Sighing, she reached her hand toward the silver coffeepot and poured her third cup of coffee.

When she was finished, she decided that she would have a shower before Marie's return. The maid had insisted that she wait so that she might help Wyeth into the shower. "Sorry, Marie, I feel good enough to take my own shower. I hope you won't be angry with me." She muttered this as she struggled into her robe, letting her toes squiggle into the plush carpet underfoot.

The old gold coloring of the tiled bathroom was warm and inviting. The room itself was large, with a shower stall separate from the sunken oval-shaped tub that four persons could have sat in without crowding. Wyeth looked at the tub with regret, promising herself a leisurely soak that evening. Still, she was very content with the long steaming shower she allowed herself, letting the hot needles of water massage away the soreness of her hip, which often bothered her at first rising. She shampooed the

25

short curling blond hair, remembering what the hairdresser who had styled its wispy beginnings after the bandages had been removed from her head had said.

"With this cut, Mrs. MacLendon, you just let the sun or an infrared lamp dry it. Towel almost dry first . . . then hand-fluff it under the lamp. You can brush it after to make it smooth . . . or, if you prefer, just poke at it with one of these long-toothed combs . . . like an Afro comb. It will curl in little tendrils all over your head. Don't look like that . . . it will be pretty, I promise . . ."

Toweling her head in front of the small dressing-room table with the long narrow wall mirror now beclouded with steam, she glanced at the serviceable steel wristwatch. Twelve twenty-five. She had been in the shower almost an hour. Well, she shrugged to herself, the sense of well-being she had was worth the time. She shook her dampened hair, pleased to find a red lamp in the ceiling. Wyeth tried the wall switches until she found the one that activated the ceiling fixture. She stood there, reveling in the heat, her fingers plumping her hair as she twisted her head back and forth. It surprised her when she gazed at her watch again that the red lamp treatment had taken her twenty minutes. Wyeth smiled to herself as she thought of Marie. The maid would probably think she had drowned. Still she didn't hurry, exulting in the languorous feeling that had been so alien to her of late.

Wrapping one of the huge gold Turkish towels around her body, she tucked it in under one arm so that it hung from her breasts much like a sarong. As she walked barefoot into the bedroom, humming to herself, Wyeth thought she heard a movement in the sitting room.

"Did you think I was never coming out, Marie?" Wyeth called.

"As a matter of fact, I have been waiting over an hour. I'm a very busy man."

The sardonic baritone voice preceded Colin MacLendon into

the bedroom by seconds. He lounged against the door frame that barely fitted his tall, muscular body.

"What—what are you doing here? I thought you were Marie, come to take the dishes away."

"Marie has been here and gone . . ."

Wyeth stiffened under the head-to-toe scrutiny that Colin MacLendon subjected her to.

". . . but, before we talk, perhaps you should dress first, not that you don't look very fetching, Aunt, but I wouldn't want you to catch cold." His eyes ran over her again in leisurely assessment before he turned and left, pulling the sitting-room door closed behind him.

Wyeth swept an angry hand over her tightening blond curls. She fought against the surge of helplessness that threatened to overcome her. She gritted her teeth, forcing her mind from the daze that it would seek if she wasn't on her guard. Dress. That was the first thing to do. The action of donning the denim wraparound skirt with matching vest and creamy beige silk shirt that matched the stitching on the denim took minutes, but it allowed her mind to clear and make her think of the man in the other room. Her temper started to smoke. How dare that insufferable, arrogant man come into her room as though he had a perfect right to do so. She should have thrown a shoe at him.

Shoes! Where were her shoes? She scrambled around on her knees, searching out the shoes that had somehow walked under the bed. Rushing too much, she snagged the blue tights she had hurriedly yanked on. She found her pumps and slipped into them. Standing in front of the mirror she took deep breaths, frowning at the five-foot-nine-inch, somewhat-too-thin woman who looked back at her. She was glad of the two-inch heels on the shoes. They would give her the added confidence she needed to face the pompous Goliath in the other room. She fluffed her hair with her hands and wished for the hundredth time that she didn't have the black smudges under her eyes or the hollows under her cheekbones. *Ah, well, I'm more filled out than I was a month ago,* she consoled herself. A quick slash of lipstick and her hand was on the door. She watched Colin MacLendon uncoil himself from the fireplace chair and approach her.

"Come and sit by the fire, Mrs. MacLendon, and tell me how you came to be married to my uncle." His words were not harsh, but Wyeth had the distinct feeling that she was on trial.

She buckled into the appointed chair, staring into the fireglow. She outlined in as few words as possible all that had happened in the past two years.

"And you've just had another skin-graft operation?" he quizzed. At her nod he continued his rapid-fire questions. "And did you not love my uncle? What am I to call you? Aunt Wyeth? Why was I not informed of this at my uncle's funeral?"

Anger simmered to the surface again, steadying her voice and her nerves. "Which question would you like answered first? Or perhaps I can answer them all as fast as you asked them. Yes. Wyeth. Mr. Wingate did tell you about me."

"Not how young you are," he cracked back.

". . . and that I was still too weak to come to the funeral." She concluded as though she hadn't spoken, her hands beginning to slip with moisture.

"Yes, he did say that," he conceded, his eyes going from her face to her clenched hands. "Still, I assumed that you were older. I realize now that the accident was more serious than I thought. I knew that my uncle had known your family for a long time."

"Your uncle and my father were college friends. He was also my godfather." She grated, hating that narrowed look on his face.

"Wingate should have told me you were a babe in arms."

"Mr. MacLendon," she began in measured tones. "I am twenty-seven and in no need of a keeper, especially you. I need nothing from you or your family." She lifted her chin and looked straight at him.

"Wrong." He answered, tilting his head and stroking his beard, but not trying to break the eye contact. "You have twenty-three percent of the shares of Montbel. That's a hell of a lot of voting power, Auntie."

"Don't be so caustic, Mr. MacLendon," she snapped, feeling perspiration bead her lip. "I know what I have. I fully intend to see that Nathaniel's wishes are carried out in regards to Montbel."

"Then, you'll turn your voting rights over to me," he barked. "That's the way Nate handled it." He straightened up from the mantel, watching her. "You're ill, aren't you?" He clasped her damp hands in his. "Come. I'll take you back to your bedroom."

"No." Wyeth tried to free her hands. "I'm all right. I get this way if I don't stay calm. It will pass soon. I'll be completely well in a few months. Then this won't happen anymore."

"Why in hell did you drive from Montreal?" he growled, sitting down in the chair opposite her. "I could have picked you up in the plane."

Wyeth ignored him, sitting back and closing her eyes, one hand pressed against her mouth.

"Here, sip some of this. It's ice water." He held the glass to her lips. "Perhaps you should go back to bed."

"No. I won't. I've been in bed most of the last two years. I'm on the mend. Just ask your Dr. Tiant. I don't intend to do anything strenuous, but I don't need to be pampered, Mr. MacLendon. I want to look around Montbel."

"All right. You're a very obstinate woman. I'll show you around," he said, a thread of amusement in his voice.

"I thought you were a busy man," Wyeth countered, her voice sounding reedy.

One corner of that hard mouth lifted, giving a sensual thrust to those firm lips. He knows damn well how attractive he is, she thought, irritation digging at her. No doubt he fancies himself a real tomcat. She looked away from those luminous green eyes, wishing he would leave. He made her uncomfortable.

"I'll always make time for my . . . aunt. We MacLendons are a very close-knit family." He almost lifted her from the chair as she started to rise. "As long as you insist on seeing Montbel, we'll take a quick tour, and then I'll bring you back here to rest."

She felt a flash of anger that he should mention her taking a nap even though she knew she would have to take one.

He held the door for her, smiling, as though he'd read her mind. "If you feel up to it, you can eat downstairs tonight. Our dining room is famous. Even the members of the MacLendon family who have houses nearby come to dine."

"How nice for you!" Wyeth said in a saccharine voice. "A gaggle of family every night."

His chuckle had a rich timbre and sent a frisson of warmth up her spine. "*Ménage à famille* can be boring, I must admit."

Taking her arm and tucking it into his, he led her out into the hall, which led to an open mezzanine area. Wyeth gasped. "It's beautiful."

They looked out across the main lobby from the second level. There were two more levels above them with circular balconies that skirted the mammoth room below. Four wings went out to form the four levels like the shape of an *X*, spreading from the main circular structure. The open center, which was the round main building, was the equivalent of six stories to the conical roof. In the center of the huge lobby a hexagon-shaped fireplace could have accommodated ten persons at each of its six sides. It rose the full six flights to the roof. The crackling blaze looked like it should have been fed whole giant oaks.

Wyeth had no idea of the passing time as her eyes wandered over the rough-hewn beauty of Montbel. It startled her when Colin's beard brushed her cheek as he leaned down to whisper to her. "There are six-million board-feet of logs at Montbel. To the MacLendon Family the number six is lucky, so you'll notice that the number will crop up now and then."

"I see," Wyeth said, edging free of the hand touching her back. He could damn well think again if he had any ideas about the direction this relationship was going to take, she vowed. She remembered all too well Harry's unfaithfulness during her illness, before Nathaniel took over her life. He hadn't hurt her deeply—she hadn't loved Harry enough for that. But it had made her wary.

"There are sporting events for every taste," he continued, the thread of amusement in his voice telling her that he had noticed her withdrawal. "We have our own beauty shop, nightclub, and ballroom. There are eight indoor tennis courts and five outdoor, an Olympic-size pool with three diving areas, plus two outdoor pools, and the river for water skiing. There is also a curling barn, thirty miles of charted cross-country skiing, downhill skiing with a championship slalom course. Impressed, Auntie?"

"It's quite beautiful, and I like what I see, but I'm afraid I'll prove to be a disappointment to you . . . Nephew," she crooned. His face was expressionless, but Wyeth's skin tingled as though she had had a mild electric charge. Almost as if she were a tuning fork to his insides, Wyeth sensed his building anger. She didn't give a damn.

"Why is that?" He threw the question like a harpoon, rolling a thin black cigar between his hands.

"I'm not much impressed by . . . things," she said, amazed by her own words. She had wanted to insult him, not bare her soul, she thought, biting her lip. She turned her back to him, ambling along the mezzanine, still looking down to the lobby. She felt a fool. "It really is an incredible place. I'm sorry I missed walking through the front entrance. That must have been a heart stopper."

"I hope you won't be upset . . . Auntie, when I tell you that I brought you into the château through the basement service entrance where the food and barrels of beer are delivered." His voice was rough velvet.

Wyeth's tart retort warred with her sense of humor. The humor won as a laugh escaped her. She turned to look at that harsh face and watched his lips quiver, then curve into a full grin. The green glitter of his eyes made her feel as though she had just run up a steep hill.

31

"You should laugh more often, *petite Tante*," he said, the deeper brown-hued eyebrows veeing upward almost to the lighter-colored hairline. Wyeth noticed how his hair caught the light from the skylight, highlighting the chestnut tint. "Shall we start again? I would like to call you Wyeth, and I want you to call me Colin."

"All right," she concurred, but still she noted his insistence on telling her rather than asking her. She didn't like it, but she let it pass. She didn't want to quarrel with him when she was trying to see Montbel. She looked away from him again.

A large hand cupped her elbow, and he led her into an old-fashioned–looking elevator, which surprised her by running like a modern one, quiet and rapid. It opened to what, Wyeth was sure, was the basement. The walls were fieldstone.

Colin led Wyeth into the rathskeller. The bar was small and compact, with bottles and glasses lining the back wall. Four high stools sat in front. At the back of the room was another walk-in fireplace, its leaping flames mesmerizing. The floors were of the same stone as the walls, worn smooth by countless patrons. Instead of being dreary the room had a cozy, protected feel to it. Wyeth was fascinated with the skis, toboggans, and bobsleds hanging from the walls and ceiling. Round oak tables and chairs were scattered here and there. There were a few people in après-ski boots lounging near the fire. They all waved to Colin and studied Wyeth.

They left and went to the nightclub, now dark and empty. "There," he said, switching on the light and pointing to the stage, where a dance band would play later in the evening.

At each and every place along the spacious corridor, Colin greeted people in fluent French. Wyeth had the sudden wish that she had studied that language rather than German.

She saw the beauty shop and was introduced to the birdlike proprietor, who ran an experienced eye over Wyeth's cropped blond curls. François had five lovely helpers who smiled and flirted with Colin and ignored Wyeth totally. The man's a damned sultan, she thought, amusement battling with contempt. After assuring François that she would come to him when she wanted her hair done, she followed Colin to the game room, with six regulation-size pool tables with orange baize tops and six smaller bumper pool tables with matching tops. Stone floors and walls were in every area.

She looked up to find Colin watching her. "Is something wrong?"

"Nothing. I want to make sure you're not tiring," he stated.

"I'll tell you when I'm tired," she snapped, biting down hard on her lip. Damn the man for patronizing her.

"So you've told me . . . a number of times. Still, I think you would be better if you returned to your room—"

"What's next?" Wyeth snapped the question at him. "If you're too busy to show me, perhaps one of the staff could do it."

She thought he was about to reply, but his jaw tightened in a stern expression as he reached out for her arm.

"We'll go through the tunnel to the pool area," he said finally in a controlled tone. "After that we'll go to the curling barn. If you're up to it, we can climb Montbel before dinner. It's only a five-hour ski down."

"Thank you. Sounds great," Wyeth shot back, disliking the man more every minute. How could he be related to Nathaniel?

They were silent as they wended their way through the curving tunnel lined on both sides with hissing steam pipes. Colin's explanation about the separate generating plant was curt and to the point. He also changed his mind about visiting the pool first and led her through a door into the curling barn. It was cold.

Wyeth was going to refuse the jacket he placed around her shoulders, but when she looked up at the dark anger in his eyes, she changed her mind.

Wyeth watched the ice game with the round granite stones that were skidded down the ice, preceded by a person sweeping with a broom. Depending on the motion of the sweeper, the stone was either hurried or slowed on its path down the ice alley. She tried to keep her mind on the action in order to better understand the game, but the man standing close at her side unnerved her. She felt out of balance, and this annoyed her. After months of painful rehabilitation she had succeeded in almost bringing herself back to her normal level of self-confidence. Now this man was jarring her loose from her foundation again. She detested the way he made her feel.

"Would you like to try curling one day?" His voice was as chilly as the barn itself.

"Yes. I think I would . . . but not today," she answered, her tones frigid.

"I wasn't implying that you begin now . . ."

"I realize that." Wyeth sighed, wishing she hadn't accompanied him.

"Look," he began, putting his hands on her shoulders to turn her to face him, "I know you've been through an ordeal. I talked to Wingate on the phone last night. He told me what happened." His gaze dissected her, picking her brain as though it were a vegetable garden, Wyeth was sure. "You're welcome to stay here and convalesce. This is your home, too."

"Even if I decide not to sell my share of Montbel to you?"

Colin stiffened, his hands clenching into her flesh. "Even then. Come through this door. The pool is down this other corridor." His voice was flat.

Wyeth shivered, sensing the force within him, like a caged, pacing tiger. "This is quite a maze. I wouldn't want to try this without a guide," she ventured, not looking at him, but seeing that grave face in front of her eyes anyway.

"You wouldn't get lost. Notice the color-coded lines on the walls. They lead to corresponding areas, such as the Green Wing, Red Wing, and so forth. The black line leads to the lobby. At every junction in the tunnel is an explanation of the color code and directions on how to use it."

"I still have the feeling that I could wander down here forever,

34

perhaps even meet the Minotaur." She tried to laugh, not quite suppressing another shudder.

"I'd come looking for you. I'd find you."

Wyeth felt the threat even as she lifted her head to look at him. Their breathing seemed to echo loud around them. She tried to look away from him, but she couldn't. She had the feeling he was surrounding her, like a black cape. She gulped air.

"Your tongue cuts like a scythe, but your body is fragile." He spoke in an absent way, his eyes running over her.

"Don't be ridiculous. I'm five-foot-seven," she croaked, taking a step backward.

His arm coiled around her, lifting her back, his mouth coming down from a great height. His lips kneaded her surprised mouth further open, his tongue touching her inner mouth until it found her tongue. Shock held her motionless, shock at her own instant response. Her heart seemed to thunder in her ears, so that she heard nothing but the roaring. She thought she heard her name groaned near her ear, but she wasn't sure. She clutched at his shoulders, knowing she'd fall without him. She tried to force herself to pull away, but instead her hands slid upward around his neck. They seemed to sway closer to each other.

From a great distance she heard the laughing voices, but when Colin pulled back from her, it angered her. He took hold of her upper arms, steadying her when she stumbled, the hawk look of him more pronounced as he watched her.

She looked away from him, not wanting him to see how dazed she was. She tried to pull her hand from his as he guided her away from the voices, but he wouldn't release her, his long strides making her run.

He pushed open a door, and at once the pungent, chlorinated smell pierced her haze and jogged her memory. She tried to turn away from the nightmarish thoughts that crowded her, but Colin led her forward. God, how often the dream of burning to death had been accompanied by the surrealistic picture of herself, goggles and team suit on, diving into a pool of fire. She had become

35

almost paranoid at the thought of swimming again because of that nightmare. She looked around her, telling herself it was a familiar, innocuous scene.

"Why are you trembling, Wyeth?" Colin leaned down to her, his one arm going around her.

"It's nothing, really. I can't explain." She inhaled deeply and looked again at the high vaulted room that was also sided in dark-hued logs. The steep pitched roof had Plexiglas panels colored a sea green that would slide down in summer to let in the warm sun. No flake of snow would cling to that sharp-angled roof, which now refracted the winter sun in warm green swatches along the surrounding wide wooden deck.

How could she explain to him that it was another pool in Quebec that she saw, the Olympic pool in Montreal as it was when she and others contended in the Summer Olympic Games. She could still see her father and her mother, red-faced and cheering. Would Colin understand about the endless practice sessions when her father would stand there, stopwatch in hand, while Wyeth strove to whittle down her times? Or would he be like Harry, who gave her polite, blank attention—like Harry who sent flowers but never came to see her or showed anything but relief when she returned his ring before marrying Nathaniel? She blinked, trying to erase memories that crowded too close. She inhaled the chlorine and saw herself in the pool working on stroke and turn, honing her flips, front and back, to razor sharpness. Swimming ten thousand meters to build endurance. How disappointed her parents were when she eschewed championship swimming for law school.

Wyeth could still feel the relief she experienced once she started law school. There had always been the fear that her parents' pressure would turn her away from her chosen career. God, that hideous nightmare . . . even in the bright of day it was there. Would she ever get over the terror that threatened to overtake her whenever she thought of swimming again? Wyeth wasn't even aware that she was trembling until Colin's arms came around her.

"What is it?" His voice harshened with concern. "I'm a damn fool. I've let you do too much."

Before Wyeth could answer him he had bent over her and swept her high into his arms. "Don't struggle. I'm not letting you walk. Besides, you're light as a feather to carry. Don't worry, I'll take you up the private elevator. No one will see you."

"But won't someone see us in the hall?" Wyeth sputtered, hating the effect his closeness was having on her. That plus the usual weakness she experienced if she was on her feet too long were making her too vulnerable to Colin MacLendon. "Could you just set me down now?" she asked as they stepped from the elevator on her floor.

"No," he growled, looking down at her in fixed concentration. "I'm not going to let you go." He paused while she lifted her key from her bag, then leaned down to let her insert it. "There. Now shall I undress you?"

"Don't be ridiculous," Wyeth snapped, looking not at him but at the door leading to the hall.

"I'm not leaving until you're in bed. Call me. I'll be in the sitting room." He spun on his heel and was through the room before a slack-jawed Wyeth could react.

"Conceited idiot, that's what he is," Wyeth muttered, aware she was being a little ungracious, but not caring. "That man is a menace." She climbed into the king-size bed, wearing just bikini briefs. She glared at the door that led into the sitting room. "I'm in bed, so you can go now," she called, hoping he would use the sitting-room door that opened into the corridor.

He put his head around the door and looked at her glowering face, the sheet pulled up to her chin, then smiled as though he could read her mind. "You look comfortable, but you should really try to think of something pleasant so that you can get that frown off your face. A sour outlook will keep you from sleeping."

"Then leave." Wyeth clipped. "That should make me smile."

His eyes darkened to a hue that reminded Wyeth of being deep in a forest. In slow measured steps he approached her bed. "Did anyone ever tell you that you have a nasty tongue?" His voice was controlled, but the eyes sparked a threat. He sat down on the bed next to her, looking first at her hands that clutched the sheet, then downward as though he could easily see through the sheet.

Wyeth steeled herself not to move to the other side of the bed, sure that that would precipitate action from him. She cursed herself for not putting on one of the nightgowns she had brought. "I am tired, so if you wouldn't mind . . ." She let her voice trail as he lifted his eyes again to her face.

"All right. You need to rest, but I refuse to let you get away with carping at me. First I retaliate, then you rest," he murmured, his eyes on her lips.

"Retaliate? What in—" Wyeth expostulated, lifting her head from the pillow too fast and forgetting to grip the sheets. The silken material slid from her body like water from a tipped plate. Her scrambling hands weren't allowed to reclaim the cover. She watched, fascinated as he studied her, two slashes of red creeping up his cheekbones.

"You are a very lovely woman," he said huskily, his head bending over her body to press his warm mouth against the hollow between her breasts.

Wyeth's cry of protest crumbled into a groan as she felt his tongue touch one rosy tip and tease it in circles. She felt her breasts harden as her hands came up to ward him off, then stayed clenched on his shoulders as he ministered to the other breast.

She felt his hand sweep downward against the covers, and she knew that her hips were bare. She felt the same hand lift her body, and she gasped as she felt his tongue at her navel. Heat shards were cutting through her in whole new sensations. She heard a sighing and realized it was her self. She wanted to stop him but found that she was kneading and stroking the heavy muscles of his shoulders and back with fevered intensity.

38

"Mrs. MacLendon?" Marie's voice was accompanied by a soft tattoo on the door. "Are you sleeping? May I come in and set out your clothes?"

Wyeth lay there gasping, her head turned into her pillow, not able to respond.

Colin rolled from the bed to his feet, one hand smoothing the hair that Wyeth's restless hands had tangled. He opened the door a crack and spoke to Marie.

Wyeth was fighting to control herself and didn't hear what was said. When Colin walked back to the bed, his face and eyes were expressionless, not missing how her hands trembled as she clutched the sheet to her once more.

"I told Marie to come back in an hour. That should give you time to rest, then she'll help you dress and show you to the dining room."

Damn the man, he was as cool as snow, not a quiver to show that they were just on the brink of making love, Wyeth thought in grating anger. "Thank you very much. I'd like to rest."

His smile was slow in coming, his brows arching in the same slow cadence. "Would you, now?" His smile deepened as he watched the color stain her neck and cheeks.

"Yes, I would," she shot back, wishing she had the strength to wipe that white grin off his handsome face.

"I'll see you later." He leaned down and gave her a hard kiss on the mouth.

"We'll see about that," Wyeth mumbled, punching at her pillow, willing herself not to think of that kiss that sundered her control and rendered her boneless. She intended to avoid him like the plague in the future. She felt the overpowering weariness that told her she had overdone it. She took a deep breath and was asleep almost at once.

Wyeth opened her eyes, feeling refreshed; newly formed scar tissue caused some aches, but still her body felt renewed. She had slept deeply, without any nightmares of swimming, or worse, the accident. She sighed, wondering what time it was, when Marie stepped from her bathroom into the bedroom, the sound of running water behind her.

"Ah, so you are awake, madame, *hein*? It is good. It is already six o'clock."

Wyeth gasped and looked at her wristwatch for confirmation, then looked back at Marie. "I've slept for three hours! You should have wakened me."

"Oh, no, madame." Marie shook her head in ponderous rhythm. "Monsieur Colin said that you were to rest. That he would make the reservation for dinner when I called him, madame."

"I see," Wyeth answered, not understanding at all, but feeling unable to cope with the indomitable Marie. She allowed herself to be led to the bathroom and watched as the young woman put bottles surrounding the bath, then began, in a ritualistic manner, to pour and shake the contents into the water. Wyeth had the giddy feeling that she was about to become part of an elaborate stew as she lowered herself into the fragrant tub.

"Ah, so relaxing for you, eh, madame? You rest. I will be back to wash you." Marie raised her hand to forestall what Wyeth was trying to say. "Monsieur Colin says that I must take care of you, madame. See, there is your oh-so-beautiful blue dress that I have hung in here to steam. Steaming velvet is so good for it, madame. Now I must call Monsieur Colin and tell him that it will be all right to have cocktails at seven." She had clasped her hands in front of her in steepled fashion. Then she looked down at Wyeth buried in bubbles to her neck. "Is it not *romantique* of Monsieur Colin to tell the family that the cocktail and dinner hours would be at your convenience, madame?" A beatific smile closed Marie's eyes, so she didn't see the look of horror on Wyeth's face.

"He didn't?" Wyeth whispered, squeezing the Loofa as though it were Colin's neck.

"Ah, but he did, madame. Monsieur Colin is a true *bon-homme*." Marie sighed and left the room.

"Yes, isn't he?" *The rat! Getting the whole family on my case the first evening I meet them,* she swore to herself. *Damn the man.* Wyeth slapped her hand downward. Bath bubbles rose in clouds onto her face making her sputter and close her eyes.

"Here, let me help you." The deep-timbred voice laughed down at her, sending a shiver of excitement through her.

She catapulted to a sitting position, her eyes shut tight. "What the hell are you doing in my bathroom? Get out of here. Ohhh, I've got soap in my eye." One hand reached out in frantic search for a towel. She pulled back when she felt the soft swipe of someone doing the job for her. "Stop that. Go away. What if Marie should return and find you here? Dammit, you've got soap in my mouth. Stop laughing."

"Then, stop wriggling. You're as slippery as a wet seal. There. Now try opening your eyes. Both of them," he said, his voice caressing.

When Wyeth squinted up at him, she realized why his voice had that sensual slur to it. He was looking down at her body where the bath bubbles had melted away from her breasts, leaving the pink-tipped fullness open to his gaze. She slid farther down into the water, breaking the spell. He looked up into her defiant face, his smile mocking.

"You have a lovely body. I love your breasts. They fit beautifully into my—"

"Stop that, and get out of here," Wyeth said bitingly. "Marie will be back any moment. She went to call—" Wyeth looked at him, mouth agape.

"I take it that seven is fine for cocktails? Then, I had better help you out of there before you're late." His voice and eyes mocked her.

Wyeth could feel herself start to redden at his intent gaze, but she fought it. Damn the man! She was not about to let him see she was disconcerted by his assessment. "I won't be late if you leave now and let me dress. It bores me to have people cluttering up my bathroom. I'm not interested in communal living."

41

"Don't be late. I'll come looking for you," he warned, then left, letting her know by his stiff back that her words angered him.

By the time Marie returned, Wyeth was sitting wrapped in a towel before the vanity doing her nails. The young woman frowned at her, berating her for not waiting for her, only slightly mollified when Wyeth pointed out how time was flying.

"Monsieur Colin was not in his office when I called, madame," Marie stated as she frowned into the mirror while brushing Wyeth's hair dry. "It is all right though, because his secretary, Yvonne Theobald, who is also my cousin, said that she would tell the family." Her hands rubbed Wyeth's scalp. "It is funny that Monsieur Colin was not there. I do not know where he could have been. Yvonne did not know, either," Marie mused as she lifted Wyeth's dress from its hanger.

"Tell me, Marie, how many of the family will be dining together tonight?" Wyeth said, trying to distract the maid from her train of thought.

"Oh, as to that, madame, it could be any number. It is always different. At Christmastime—well, that is something. They all come. *Mon Dieu!* do they come," she exclaimed, throwing her one arm wide as she stood back to look at Wyeth. "Tonight I know for sure that there will be Amalie Colbert, Tante Amalie, but you must not call her that. She is Monsieur Colin's aunt but close to him in age, you understand. She was stepsister to his sainted mother. Then there will be Cecile MacLendon, who is very little, very old, and very formidable, madame." She leaned forward to pluck at the fullness in Wyeth's gown. "It is good that your dress covers your scar, madame. Such pain you must have had."

"Yes, but it's almost gone now."

"Ah, *oui,* that is good." She smiled, then continued telling Wyeth about the family when she was prodded by her. "Well, Monsieur Luc Colbert is coming tonight. He comes quite often, even though he is a lawyer working in Montreal. Dr. Émile, who

42

took care of you, will be here, as will his wife, Madame Solange, who is Monsieur Colin's sister. I am not sure of any others, madame." Marie shrugged, her face expressive.

Wyeth stood in front of the three-way mirror that Marie had opened for her. It was recessed into the wall, and Wyeth knew that she would never have found it had not Marie shown it to her. She heard Marie's admiring sigh behind her.

"Oh, madame, you look like one of our Christmas angels, to be sure."

Wyeth stared into the mirror at the too-slim woman in the mid-calf-length sky blue velvet dress that echoed the color of her eyes. The dress fell in very soft, but not full, folds from under her bust, touching at her narrow hips, then falling free to a slightly uneven hemline that dipped lower in the back, emphasizing her long, well-shaped legs. Her hair was a nimbus of gold curls that framed the delicate bones of her face. The slim neck and shoulders rose porcelain clear from a softly rounded neckline. The simple but exquisite cut of the gown enhanced the delicate look she had so recently acquired, giving her an almost ethereal appearance.

Marie handed her her bag at just five minutes before the hour.

"Would you show me to the sitting room, Marie?" Wyeth asked, wanting to beg Marie to stay with her.

Instead of answering Wyeth the young woman turned away to answer the knock on the hallway door. "Ah, good evening, monsieur. Madame, here is Monsieur Colin to show you the way."

Colin didn't move from the doorway as Marie disappeared around him. His eyes touched each part of her as if to caress her. Wyeth took a deep breath and looked at him in a bold, assessing way, trying to ignore the banked fire in those green orbs.

He was wearing a deep-brown velvet jacket that echoed his chestnut hair and beard, sharpening the copper highlights. The suede seemed stretched over his wide shoulders, his tan wool slacks forming to his narrow hips and muscular legs with tai-

43

lored fit. He looked altogether too masculine, too overpowering, like a man who spent most of his time out in the forest hunting some dangerous prey. Not at all a business magnate, Wyeth thought waspishly. How she wished he didn't look as though he were reading her mind. Her gaze dropped to the florist box in his hand.

"Here. This is for you, for your first night at Montbel. Shall I pin it on for you?" he quizzed, the mocking smile deepening as she stiffened.

"No, thank you. I would rather do it myself." She didn't want him closer than arm's length. She hated the weakness that caused her to tremble as she pinned the single orchid to her dress.

"You look like Venus rising from the sea, Wyeth." He spoke just behind her, his gaze glittering as he watched her in the mirror. Wyeth fancied she could see green devils dancing in his eyes.

He turned her in a slow circle toward him, his hands spanning her waist. The kiss was a sudden, gentle brush of lips that threatened to disarm her. "Every woman in the dining room will be jealous of you, *ma belle*. Every man will envy me. Come, we'll join the others."

Before they left the room, Wyeth looked again at the creamy orchid with the deeper cream center that Colin had given her. "Thank you for this. It's quite beautiful."

Colin took her hand, entwining his fingers with hers, pulling her close to his side as they left the room to walk around the balcony overlooking the lobby and the stairs. People were standing around the mammoth fireplace as they descended together, having drinks in crystal stemware that was lifted from trays held by liveried waiters. "Why are you looking so withdrawn, Wyeth? Would you have preferred to have cocktails with the guests rather than the family?" he quizzed, piercing her mind again.

"Don't be silly. I'm here to meet the family, aren't I?" she

44

replied almost too sharply. She wanted to show him he couldn't read her thoughts at all when he gave her that knowing grin.

"Don't be uncomfortable about it," he whispered, squeezing her hand tighter when she attempted to pull free. "There are many times when I prefer strangers to my family, but then there are times when I enjoy being with them, as I'm going to enjoy it when I introduce you to them." His laugh puzzled and alarmed her, but he didn't elaborate.

People hailed Colin when they reached the lobby, staring at Wyeth. Colin answered them all but didn't pause. He turned away from the main section of the lobby to lead her down a shorter hall leading to a double-doored room. One of the doors was open, and Wyeth could hear the murmur of voices coming from it. She hesitated, swallowing the saliva that seemed too much for her mouth.

Colin gave her a lopsided smile that didn't soften the hard planes of his face, then lifted one arm to usher her into the room.

She felt that she had stepped into a circle of silence, the others in the room seeming to move in slow motion as they turned toward her.

"*Cher frère,* you didn't tell us she was beautiful, neither did that husband of mine," pouted the impish-looking girl-woman who stepped forward, her hand outstretched. She grasped Wyeth's hand with both of hers. "You are Wyeth. But how silly of me to tell you that. You already know who you are, don't you? I am Solange, your niece, if you can believe such an anachronism." Solange's laugh brought an answering one from Wyeth. Solange stepped back, her eyes widening. "My dear Wyeth, you are quite enchanting. She is, isn't she, *chéri?*" She pulled the object of her question forward and hooked her arm through his in loving capture.

Wyeth recognized Dr. Tiant and smiled at him, relieved to see a face she knew.

"How are you feeling, Miss Cr—er, that is, Mrs. MacLendon?" He smiled back, shrugging in a Gallic way for his mistake.

"Please call me Wyeth, Dr. Tiant. I'm just fine, thank you, very much."

"*Bien, bien.* And you must call me Émile, my dear. May I say how lovely you look this evening?"

Wyeth nodded, pleased, but feeling an unaccustomed shyness as the others pushed forward, clamoring to be introduced. She took a step back, confused, and felt a warm palm at her waist. She exhaled, feeling calmer as Colin turned her to another person. His breath feathered her forehead when he spoke.

"This is my cousin, Luc Colbert. He practices law in Montreal."

Wyeth wondered at his clipped tones for a moment, before allowing her hand to be taken by the slim, slightly built man in front of her. He had thin-faced good looks that hinted at a wiry strength. She was surprised when he lifted her hand to his lips.

"Colin no doubt wishes me back in Montreal now that he has met you, *chère Tante.*" The thin lips smiled at Colin in a veiled malice that Wyeth didn't understand. "Now that you are here, I shall be at Montbel more often. I shall take you skiing, skating, curling, or anything else that appeals to you. *You* are most appealing to me."

Wyeth could feel Colin stiffen at her side, his fingers tightening on her body, but before he could speak, a throaty voice interjected.

"Come now, Luc, do step aside so that I might view our guest of honor."

Colin reached an arm around Wyeth and past Luc to grasp the hand of one of the most doll-like women Wyeth had ever seen. Just under medium height with small bones and feet, her curvaceous figure was swathed in red chiffon, that draped from one shoulder, leaving the other bare. Her hair was Oriental black, swept back, and high on her neck in a thick twist. The face was an ivory sculpture topped by wide-apart brown eyes. The lovely creature reached up and kissed Colin full on the mouth. Colin smiled at her, then turned to Wyeth.

"This is my mother's stepsister, my *aunt* Amalie Colbert."

Wyeth glanced sideways at Colin, hearing the amusement in his voice. Amalie Colbert gave a pouting smile, but her eyes had an irritated glitter.

"Pay no attention to him, Wyeth. He says this to annoy me. I am but six months older than he himself is. So . . ." She shrugged, taking Wyeth's arm and managing to lead her away from the others. ". . . *chérie*, you have come to give us back Montbel, and then I suppose you will be on your way again. It would be dull for you here, *sans doute*, away from your circle of friends." The deep-red lips were more of a slash than a smile as she looked up at Wyeth. "It is a pity that you speak no French. For me it is so much more comfortable to converse in that language, so civilized." With a delicate movement she fitted a long brown cigarette into a gold holder. "Perhaps you could fly back to Montreal with Luc, no? He could handle the legal details of the transfer for you. I am sure he would expedite things for you. There would be release forms for you to . . ."

Wyeth could barely follow the low-voiced woman speaking so rapidly, but the import was clear. A slow heat was building in Wyeth as Amalie still continued to lead her into a secluded corner of the room. Wyeth wrenched her arm free. "I've only arrived yesterday, Miss Colbert. I would hardly think of insulting your charming family by leaving Montbel so soon. Besides, business is so boring to discuss at a family party."

Actually Wyeth had a good mind for business and wasn't bored at all. She could certainly see through Amalie's clumsy attempts to manipulate her, to simply assume that she would sign over her share of Montbel within the week and then leave. The thought peaked her suspicion. Was that Colin's intent as well, to manipulate her by using the leverage of his masculine appeal, his expert, disarming lovemaking? Was that how he hoped to secure the shares of Montbel she controlled? Quite likely, she sighed. She had to keep her eyes open here, she could see. This was no ordinary family gathering.

"*Madame* Colbert, my dear Wyeth. I am a widow. I married my cousin Paul Colbert, Luc's older brother. In our family we tend to marry our relations. Montbel holds us all. We don't encourage outsiders." A stream of smoke touched Wyeth's face before she turned away. She almost bumped into Colin in her haste to cross the room.

"What is it, Wyeth? Did Amalie say something to upset you?" His hand tightened on her arm, those green fire eyes searching her face.

"Not really," she snapped. "It was just a warning really. She's positively charming."

A gust of laughter burst from him. "I'm surprised you left her standing, *chérie.*"

"When I'm stronger, I may push her into a snow drift," Wyeth grated, trying to maneuver herself free of his arm, but not succeeding. His laughter made her fume. "I'm not turning my shares over just like that," she hissed, bunching her fists as Colin took a thin black cigar from his pocket. "And your stupid family smokes too much."

"I don't think you'll mind the aroma of this. It's a Corona Colorado Claro," Colin stated, his amusement increasing as she glared at him over the flare of the pencil-slim lighter. "When I tell you that I am not an addict but that I limit myself to one per day, will you stop glowering at me?" he drawled, his eyes still alight.

Wyeth knew he didn't give a damn if she approved of his actions or not. "I couldn't care a whit if you went up in a cloud of blue smoke. And, besides, I've already seen you smoking one of those today."

His laugh was deep and turned heads their way. He took her arm and turned her, leading her across the room, his breath brushing her neck when he spoke. "You haven't met Tante Cecile or Bill Balmain."

They stopped in front of a settee near the fireplace, where a modified Queen Victoria sat holding court, complete with black thorn stick at her side and a long, rustling black moiré dress with fine crocheted black lace on the neck and sleeves. Her blue-gray hair was curled and covered with a lace prayer cap. A tall, blond-haired, thickset man lounged against the mantel, chatting with her. When she noticed Wyeth, the crusty little monarch grabbed the walking stick and banged it on the floor.

"So, young lady, you finally deign to be introduced to me. In my day it was different. We had manners. We didn't ignore old people. What is it? Do you dislike my old-fashioned dress? Do you think I am too decrepit to carry on conversation? Well? Speak up."

Wyeth smiled. "I was thinking that you know exactly how charming you look in your Old-World dress. You and I both know that far from being decrepit, you're sharp as a tack . . . but I still won't curtsy, madame."

A hoot of laughter from the blond man, who straightened from the mantel at Wyeth's approach, was echoed by Colin's chuckle. A reluctant smile fought through Tante Cecile's frown.

Colin's arm pulled Wyeth to him as he placed a kiss behind her right ear, sending a frisson of warmth traveling up her spine. "This is Wyeth, Tante. What do you think?"

The old woman looked from Wyeth back to Colin. "I think that even you will find this angel a match *formidable*, Colin." The matriarch patted the couch at her side. "Sit here, child. Bill, you must meet our Wyeth . . ." Her pronunciation of Bill sounded like "Beel." Wyeth's name sounded like "Wyet."

The blond man bowed from the waist. "Guillaume Balmain at your service, Madame MacLendon. Everyone calls me Bill. I was a classmate of Colin's at college and work at Northern Telecom in Montreal. Now that you know everything about me, will you marry me? Anyone who can read Tante so clearly is the woman for me. You must be astute, intelligent, and not least of all, courageous to have done so. You're lovely to look at as well, but that doesn't count."

Laughter bubbled out of Wyeth as she sank down next to Tante Cecile on the brocade love seat.

The old lady patted her arm. "You must pay no attention to Bill. He is a terrible flirt."

Bill took hold of Tante's hand, lifting it to his lips. "Only with you, you tantalizing creature."

Tante Cecile tapped his leg with her walking stick, shushing him. Wyeth knew she was not at all displeased. She herself felt drawn to the laughing brown eyes of Bill Balmain.

When Colin turned away to speak with someone else, Wyeth felt a sense of loss. She had turned back to answer Tante's question when she felt a hand on her shoulder.

Luc Colbert reached down to pull her to her feet. "Come and talk to me for a moment."

Wyeth didn't know how to tell him in a polite way that she would rather stay with Tante Cecile, so she inclined her head in assent.

"Don't take her far away, Luc," Tante snapped. "She is to sit beside me at dinner."

"I will return her when she has seen our winter moon." He laughed at the frowning monarch.

Wyeth said nothing as he led her to one of the floor to ceiling French windows and swept back the heavy woven drapes. They chatted for a few moments, Luc asking about Boston and her drive from Montreal.

"Oh, but you only stayed for two days?" he said. "You must go back with me, Wyeth, and let me show you my city."

Wyeth didn't know how to answer. She found that his stare unnerved her, so she kept her eyes on the moon that hung over the ice-encrusted river. "I have seen some of it. I was there for the Olympics some years ago."

Neither of them noticed Colin until he spoke, suddenly beside her. "It's time we were going to the dining room, Wyeth."

50

"And are you our aunt's keeper, Cousin?" Luc's question had a silky menace that confused Wyeth.

"I'm escorting her to dinner. Perhaps you'll bring Amalie," Colin drawled, his eyes like agates.

Wyeth shivered as Colin put his hand on her waist.

CHAPTER THREE

Colin looked down at her as he led her along the corridor, his eyes seeming to touch every part of her face. He smiled, the crease at the side of his mouth deepening.

Other diners watched the family's descent as they came down the wide oaken stairway that split right and left halfway. It allowed a double entryway to the dining room that was both attractive and utilitarian. A balcony on the lobby level followed the contours of the spacious room, supported by coarse fieldstone pillars roughly an arm-span width. The pillars gave a measure of privacy and intimacy to the tables for two that cuddled up to each one of the pillars.

The maître d' came forward and bowed low to Tante, a warm smile on his face. He led them to an alcove not too far from another of the huge fireplaces that seemed to be a Montbel trademark. Instead of one huge table for the group, there were three round tables, each set for six.

Wyeth was between Colin and Tante Cecile, with Bill and the Tiants joining them. Another couple rushed into the room to join Luc and Amalie at their table.

"Sorry we're late, Tante, Colin. Mardi couldn't get the baby to settle down. You understand, Tante? Oh, hello. Are you Wyeth? I'm Kyle MacLendon, Colin's brother, and this is my wife, Mardi—you know, like Mardi Gras."

Wyeth smiled at Kyle and at his tiny wife, whose dark-eyed looks reminded Wyeth of Monique.

The MacLendons and the Colberts seemed to have a great deal to say to each other. They chattered without stop even as they ordered dinner. They could step in and out of each other's conversations without losing a breath or their place. Wyeth was sure she was the only confused one, her head swiveling as she tried to answer all the questions put to her. She was unprepared for the feather-light meat pie that was her appetizer. It bubbled golden on a Sevres-like plate.

She enjoyed the idea of having her own waiter and pointed to the *truite en colère,* not trusting her French to say it, but understanding enough to know she was having a dish of trout with its tail in its mouth. She acquiesced to the boning of her fish, then was amazed when the waiter lifted the skeleton clear without losing a crumb of tender flesh. He had taken her baked potato from the jacket, whipped it with cream and butter in a small copper frying pan on his trolley, then restuffed it, topped with grated cheese and grated black pepper.

"*Voilà,* madame. You will like the coating of pepper, I know. Soon you will have a Montbel appetite, madame."

Wyeth looked up at the smiling man with the shoe-button eyes and patent leather hair and nodded.

"Thank you, Marcel. Everything looks wonderful," Wyeth stated, wondering if she would be able to eat it all.

"Of course, madame. Here, let me slice you some bread. It is from our own bakery, as are all the desserts."

Colin turned to catch her eye, his grin registering her plight as she looked at the food. "Are you taking good care of Madame, Marcel?"

"Of a surety, Monsieur Colin." His tone said that he took umbrage at the question. "She needs much food. I will see to it."

Wyeth gritted her teeth, wanting to dump the boned trout into Colin's lap, as Marcel was even more attentive after Colin's question.

When she saw the dessert platters being brought by the waiters, she felt faint. Glistening like flowers on the silver tray were

53

tarts, éclairs, cream puffs, ice cream pies, fruit pies, and cakes of every description, most with whipped cream adorning the top. She demurred, ignoring the tightening of Marcel's lips.

"Do take something, *chérie*. You need fattening," Tante Cecile urged, helping herself to a cream puff.

"I haven't the room, Tante. Besides, I'm sure I gained a few pounds during this meal. I'm just glad I'm not in training anymore; I can imagine what my coach would say."

Her voice echoed in the sudden silence, it seemed to Wyeth, looking down at her clasped hands. Why had she said anything? she agonized.

"Training? What is this training, *petite*?" Tante queried.

"I don't train anymore, but when I was an undergraduate, I was on a team at UCLA." She smiled, wishing they would look at someone else. She felt Colin's fingers on her shoulders, kneading them.

Amalie's voice was clear over the murmurs of the other diners. "But, *chérie*, I, for one, am fascinated. I don't know many female athletes. Tell me, what is it that you do? Baseball? Wrestling, perhaps? Surely not your so rigorous football?" she caroled, abrading Wyeth's nerves.

"I am, that is, I was a swimmer. I also played tennis," she said, her tones firm, her chin raised just a little.

Luc pushed back his chair so that he could see around Bill. "Do I understand that when you said you came to our Olympics, you came to compete?" Luc blew a stream of smoke from the side of his mouth.

For a flash in time the question remained unanswered as Wyeth left them. She was marching around the stadium in Montreal the day after Bruce Jenner won the Decathlon. She had been a happy contender, arm in arm with the other athletes, some of them her own countrypeople, many others from different countries. She could still see the illuminated scoreboard that had said A BIENTÔT! MOSCOW. She could still remember promising herself that she would go to Moscow for the gold. Moscow had been canceled for Americans, her chance for the gold a nebulous dream. It was aeons ago, another lifetime.

"Well, Wyeth, aren't you going to answer Luc?"

"What? What did you say, Amalie?"

"Luc asked you a question." Amalie's voice was impatient.

Colin threw his crumpled napkin onto the table. "This is not an inquisition, Amalie. Perhaps Wyeth doesn't want to answer Luc."

"Protecting her again, Cousin?" Luc quizzed, his voice low, his eyes narrowed. "Or are you trying to protect your own interests in Montbel? Next you'll be telling us that you are marrying our lovely 'aunt' to protect her."

Colin's chair almost tipped backward as he surged to his feet, menace in the forward thrust of his body. "You keep your—"

Wyeth's hand closed on Colin's arm, claiming his attention. "It's all right. I'll answer. Yes, I competed in the Olympics. My best placement was eighth in the two-hundred meter freestyle. I also swam backstroke and came in eleventh." Her voice was flat, the words clicking together like a recorded message.

Tante Cecile banged her stick on the floor. "Enough of this. I wish to go back to the sitting room. Come here to me, Colin; I wish to take your arm."

Much of the rest of the evening had blurred edges. Wyeth had the feeling that she had stepped through Alice's looking glass when she had involved herself with the MacLendons. She thought of Luc as the Cheshire Cat, Bill as the Rabbit. Amalie as the Queen of Hearts? Wyeth gave herself a mental shake and tried to listen to Kyle and Mardi as they told about the house they were building.

"We want it to be like Colin's house, but of course it will be smaller. Some time you must have Colin take you up the mountain to see his house, Wyeth. It's worth the trip, isn't it, Kyle?"

Wyeth smiled at Kyle when he endorsed his wife's remark, liking the two young people who were so much in love.

As everyone wended their way in slow fashion back to the

sitting room, Amalie came up next to Wyeth, her jeweled fingers touching Wyeth's arm.

"You have captivated Montbel. *Quelle surprise, eh, chérie!* How foolish of our dear Luc to mention marriage in connection with you and Colin, was it not?" Amalie purred.

"Don't concern yourself, Amalie. It was just a bad joke," Wyeth said, her voice cutting.

A streak of red tinged the cheekbones of the other woman, her eyes fixing on Wyeth. "A sad joke, I would say, considering what an albatross you seem to be to those around you."

"What are you trying to say?" Wyeth choked, the palms of her hands beading in moisture, her stomach churning.

Amalie's shrug spoke volumes. "How is it that you seem to survive but bring misfortune to others, eh? What of your parents and our poor Nate? *Quel dommage, hein?*" She drifted away, her perfume wafting around Wyeth.

"They were accidents . . ." Wyeth whispered, her voice reedy and almost inaudible. She felt the others moving around her as she stood there clenching and unclenching her fists.

The French were known to be superstitious, but Wyeth realized Amalie's insult had only upset her so much because it put into words the deep and unspoken fear that sometimes plagued her. "Damn superstitious nonsense!" she muttered, her hands still icy cold.

Bill Balmain spoke to her twice before she was aware of him. "What is it, Wyeth? Did Amalie say something to shock you? You mustn't mind her, you know. She grows claws when another beautiful woman is around. She hates competition, and you have been taking Colin's attention away from her. She thinks of Colin as her own." Bill grinned at her, squeezing her arm, but his eyes were concerned.

Luc came up on Wyeth's other side. "I couldn't help overhearing that remark about Amalie and Colin. My dear Bill, surely you haven't forgotten how inseparable they have always been. Remember how they were when they were at McGill!"

"That was fifteen years ago, Luc," Bill said, his tones dry.

Wyeth wasn't listening to them. She couldn't stop thinking about what Amalie had said to her. She had never been a superstitious person, but the word went round her brain. Jinx. Could she have jinxed her loved ones? No, dammit, it was too ridiculous. She wouldn't dwell on such nonsense.

When they reached the sitting-room door, Bill and Luc were still dueling verbally. They seemed to have forgotten her presence. She held back and let the flow of people precede her into the room.

Without thinking about it she turned away from the door and walked down the corridor. She had no idea where she was heading. She saw a stairway and descended to the basement level. Wyeth could hear the cacophony coming from the nightclub as the instruments were being tuned. She went past the rathskeller unseeing. The only thing in front of her was the heavy metal doorway leading from the ski shop to the outdoors.

The blast of cold air was therapeutic. She stepped out onto the icy path, heedless of the danger of slipping with just thin-soled sandals. Her bare shoulders were assaulted by the blustery wind coming through the pines. She listened for a moment. The wind had a strange sound, like the whimpering of a dog.

Her whole body was shuddering with cold now, but Wyeth stayed still, listening to the sound. It came again, convincing Wyeth that it was an animal. She turned and crouched, trying to get in the lee of the Dumpster. At the same time she saw the cowering animal that had taken shelter behind the Dumpster. It was young, Wyeth could tell, but it was of a good size. She reached down to pet it just seconds before she was swept off her feet and carried back inside to the warm ski shop.

"Are you out of your mind, Wyeth?" Colin growled. "What the hell is the matter with you? Do you want to catch pneumonia?"

Wyeth struggled in the iron grip. "No, I don't. Let me down, Colin." Her teeth chattered, making speech difficult. "I have to get the dog. He's out there, and he's cold and hungry. I have to get him."

"Never mind the animal. My God, you're so cold," Colin growled, getting closer to the stove, setting her on her feet, and rubbing her hands.

"Colin, please." Tears welled. Wyeth bit at her lip. "Please. He's shivering; he needs help." Wyeth blinked, unable to prevent a tear from sliding down her cheek into the corner of her mouth.

Colin studied her for a moment, his eyes watchful. His one finger caught at the tear. Then he put the finger to his mouth, licking his finger.

Wyeth's heart lurched against her chest wall as she watched him.

He led her closer to the potbellied stove and reached for a blackened coffeepot. He filled a mug and handed it to her. "I'll bring the dog. Stay warm."

In a few minutes he was back, bringing the bedraggled creature into the cozy room. To Wyeth the dog looked like a large-boned German shepherd. She had always had small dogs like her miniature poodle, Tobey. The gangling creature in Colin's arms fascinated her. Its ears and eyes were too big, and there seemed to be too much of a coat for the dog inside. When Colin set the dog down, it collapsed in a heap close to the stove. Wyeth watched it shake as she tried to control the bone-wracking shivers that assailed her in spite of the heat from the stove.

"He should be fed," Wyeth stammered.

Colin's eyes were piercing, raking her from top to bottom. Then he called a man named Albert. From the back room an older man, lean and weathered-looking, with tufts of gray hair escaping from under a voyageur cap and a battered pipe clamped in his teeth, ambled toward them. Colin spoke to him in rapid French, never once taking his eyes off Wyeth. Then he handed the dog into Albert's care. Colin removed his jacket and wrapped Wyeth in it. "You're going with me, young lady."

"Where are we going? What about the dog?" Wyeth rasped.

"The dog will be fine, *petite*. He will be fed and then washed. We are going to the pool."

When Colin felt her pull back, he put his arm around her, leading her down the hall, brooking no argument. "We're not going for a swim, Wyeth. We're going to use the sauna. It will warm and relax you." He rushed her through the tunnel, only pausing to flip on the electricity for the pool area. He guided her along a damp, narrow aisle between the men's and women's locker rooms.

"Here we are, Wyeth. There are bath sheets on the shelves in the locker rooms. Can you undress, shaking like that?" A grin creased his face as she frowned at him. "I'd be glad to help."

"Then close the door behind you as you leave," she said, then sneezed, spoiling the effect of her lofty words. When she heard the door click, she sighed, leaning back against the door.

She stripped off her clothes with shaking hands, almost unable to hang the dress on the wooden hangers that had been provided.

Wrapping herself in one of the bath sheets, she came back into the hall barefoot to find Colin lounging in front of the sauna, one shoulder propped against the wall, a bath sheet wrapped around his middle.

"I didn't want you to be lonely," he stated, watching her stiffen and draw back. He cupped her elbow and opened the door all in the same motion. "It was only turned off a short time ago, so we won't have long to wait before it's at full heat."

She tried to pull back from him, his nearness making her uncomfortable, but he wouldn't release her. His hard smile told her he knew what she was thinking, so she steeled herself not to flinch when he put his arm around her to help her over the step into the sauna.

She didn't want to look at him, but she couldn't help but see how his bare chest gleamed broad and muscular in the reddish light, making the brown hair on his chest a chestnut color, the same color as on his arms and legs.

Heat from the wooden enclosure enveloped her in a soothing

59

massage. Wyeth stood still for a moment just inside the door, her hands touching the sarong-wrapped towel, checking to see that it was tucked tight between her breasts. She stepped up to the second level, sat down, and closed her eyes. The heat seeped into her pores, dispelling the chill, stopping the muscle tremors caused by the cold.

Long moments passed. The silence felt charged to Wyeth. She wished Colin would say something. Every inhaled and exhaled breath was amplified.

She cleared her throat. "It was good of you to bring the dog inside." She was aware that he was watching her as he lounged against the wooden wall. She coughed. "I could tell he was young even though he's a good size."

Colin leaned forward, his thigh brushing hers. "Wyeth, that wasn't a dog. It was a young wolf." He inclined his head at her look of disbelief. "Believe me, it was a wolf. We have many of them here in Quebec. Most Quebecois love children and animals. When they find a lost wolf cub, they often adopt it. Sometimes the animal gets too large to house and feed; sometimes they get hard to handle. Then it's released back into the wild. Most readapt to their own kind. This one probably got onto the scent of Montbel. Maybe he's more tame than some."

"You won't let me keep him," Wyeth pronounced, feeling dejected.

"You may keep him, *ma mie.*" Colin took her hand. "He's yours. What will you call him?"

Wyeth didn't hear his last question. She had such a choking feeling of happiness. It had been so long since she had felt that inner warmth that she turned to Colin without thinking, reaching up to pull his head down to kiss him on the corner of his mouth.

For a moment he was still, then he reached down and gathered her up into his arms, sweeping her from the bench to his knees. Her face was pressed for a moment against the curling hair of his chest, her mouth and nose filled with the clean masculine

60

smell of him. His hand touched her chin, bringing her face up. His mouth touched hers in gentle search, then firmed, parting her mouth to find the warm moistness of her tongue. The kiss warmed her as no sauna could have.

His seeking hands parted the toweling to cup her breasts. Wyeth reeled, unable to understand her own response. With his mouth still on hers he lifted her from his knees to place her on the wooden bench, the hard length of his body following hers. Both towels were pushed aside by his impatient hand. His mouth was everywhere, burning her breasts, her abdomen, her navel.

Wyeth wanted to push him away but felt her hands clutching his shoulders to pull him closer. She felt his hand stroking the sensitive skin of her inner thigh, and her heart beat a tattoo in her chest. He leaned over her.

An excruciating pain made her scream. Her injured hip was twisted against the wooden slats of the bench. She bit her lip hard.

Colin pulled away from her at once. "What the hell did I do to you? I've hurt you." He tried to lift her, but Wyeth shook her head, her teeth still biting into her lip.

She put her hand down and tried to lift her body free. When Colin saw what she was doing, he levered his hand beneath her and freed her.

"It's my hip," Wyeth exhaled.

Colin eased her hand away, looking at the white scar that etched a half-moon on her right hip. He knelt on the lower bench, placing his lips to the scar, at the same time covering her with the towel. "I'm sorry, *ma mie*. We'll save our lovemaking for when you're feeling better and we are both in a comfortable bed. How many others have wanted you as I do, I wonder," he muttered, kissing her knee.

Wyeth stared at him, a mixture of anger and excitement coursing through her. "Is that my cue?" she rasped. "Do I quiz you about the women you've had?" Her voice wobbled despite her best efforts to steady it. She took a quavery breath as the silence lengthened.

"Point well taken, *petite*. I have no right to ask you anything, but" —here he shrugged in a very Gallic way— "I'm a very possessive man." He knotted the towel at her breast again, letting his knuckles rest against her skin.

"Possessive? How flattering. Is all this charm designed to get me into bed or to sign over Montbel?" Wyeth quizzed. She knew his anger would surface in a rush but felt she would rather fight him this way than face the power his slightest touch seemed to have over her.

"I haven't made up my mind," he growled, the words chewed well before they were spit at her. "Perhaps *both, petite*. I would never throw you out of my bed."

"You won't get the chance," Wyeth snapped, standing on unsteady legs and trying to edge past him to the door.

A warm hand on her shoulder stopped her. "Is this another souvenir of your accident, Wyeth?" His lips touched the burn mark below her left shoulder blade, where the towel sagged down her back. She quivered at his touch, cursing her traitorous body.

"Yes. Some of that scar tissue will be removed by plastic surgery; that will be the last operation, but not for a while."

"Of course not. You'll rest here at Montbel, get your strength back, then we'll see about the operation. Now, get dressed." He looked at her, not smiling. "I can dress you if it's difficult for you."

"No. No, it isn't difficult." Wyeth wanted to ask him what he meant by *"we'll* see about the operation," but she didn't have the energy just then to handle a head-to-head argument, which she was sure would ensue. She had the feeling she would end by capitulating. She would wait until she was stronger; then she would tackle him on that possessive attitude of his.

She made a face at her crumpled underthings, but she had to

smile at the velvet dress. The steam in the locker room had conditioned it to fresh-pressed.

Pushing at her mass of tight curls with her fingertips to fluff the blond strands, Wyeth couldn't help noticing how relaxed her face looked. Her lashes flickered as she thought of her moments with Colin in the sauna. Fool! She glowered at her image. *Can't you see the way he's manipulating you? Don't let those green eyes fool you! This isn't Nate.*

With that mute pep talk she looked around the locker room to see if she had forgotten anything and spied her wilted orchid. She lifted it to put it in the trash can but found herself putting it in her small bag instead. *I'll throw it out when I get to my room,* she told herself.

Colin was standing in the hallway, legs apart, fists shoved into his trouser pockets, jacket across one shoulder. "Ready?"

"Yes, and thank you. The sauna was just what I needed," Wyeth said, her voice sounding prim to her ears; but she didn't look at Colin to see if he had the same reaction.

"I enjoyed it myself," he leaned down and whispered, his beard grazing her cheek, making her bristle and glare at him. He lifted both hands in front of him as though he were defending himself. "All right, tiger, don't tear into me. I have to get you to bed."

"I can find my own way, thank you," Wyeth answered, attempting to pull her arm free without success. When she turned to go to the elevator, Colin turned her around and led her toward the ski shop.

"Albert, Albert, where are you?" Colin called. "Ah, there you are. Where is the cub? Ah, I see. Look at him, Wyeth—there, near the stove."

Wyeth went past him to kneel in front of the sprawled dog, which gave a huge yawn. Its clean fur was fluffed up in all directions, and its tail made lazy thumps on the floor. She cradled its head in her hands, rubbing its ears. "Oh, what a nice dog you are. I'll call you Beau. Doesn't that mean handsome, Colin?" Wyeth asked, delighted with the dog.

"Yes. Beau is a good name for him," Colin spoke, coming down on his haunches to pat the dog. "You can take him to your suite if you like, Wyeth. I've had you moved to the family wing on the first floor, down the hall from the main sitting room. You'll have a private area outside your room where you can run him. I think you'll like it there." He laughed as the cub gripped his hand in strong teeth and started to chew it, growling all the while. "Tough, are you?"

Wyeth watched him as he wrestled with the dog and grudged that he was more than handsome-looking. He was probably the most attractive man she'd ever seen. The hawklike nose, the full beard, the high-planed cheekbones, were too rugged to fall into the category of classic good looks. Wyeth knew that most women would give him more than a second look, and she was sure he knew it.

He became aware of her gaze and turned to look at her, his expression veiled. He smiled at the red stain on her cheekbones. "Something wrong?" he quizzed, his voice husky.

"No." She swallowed. "I just wanted to thank you and didn't know quite how to phrase it."

"Don't worry, *ma mie*. I'll think of some way for you to repay me." He laughed out loud as she jumped to her feet, arms akimbo, glaring at him. "I'm too tired to fight with you. I'll take a rain check though." He rose in one fluid motion, still looking at her. "Tell your dog to come along. It's time you were in bed."

Wyeth did feel tired, but she would never tell him that. When she bent over the panting pup, she prayed she could get him to accompany her. She looked first at Albert, who was leaning against the stone wall worrying his old pipe in his teeth. He removed it and knocked it against his hand, nodding to her in an encouraging way.

At the first whistle Beau cocked his head, watching Wyeth. She clapped her hands, urging also with her voice. In a few seconds he rose and came to her, trying to bite her sandals. Wyeth felt a burst of pride as the pup ambled after her into the corridor.

Albert's rapid spate of French followed her, making Colin laugh. "Albert says that your Beau is a pig and will eat Montbel into the poorhouse."

Wyeth gave a sniff, directed at the phlegmatic Albert, and turned away laughing.

For the short moment her eye was off Beau, he tried to scamper into the open elevator. Wyeth made a grab for his loose fur, collaring him. "I'm sure Albert is wrong about Beau," she puffed, trying to make him heel. "I'm sure Beau has lovely manners. He's just a little too enthusiastic. Heel, Beau. Be a good boy," Wyeth panted.

Colin's laugh made her grit her teeth as she struggled with the exuberant cub. He made no move to help her until Beau jumped on one of the bejeweled guests exiting from the nightclub.

"My dear Mr. MacLendon, I had no idea you had a dog. Perhaps my poor Frou-Frou could accompany me sometime."

"Oh no, Mrs. Castleman. Beau is a—that is—we are training him as a guard dog," Colin replied, giving Wyeth a murderous look when she giggled, his face reddening from trying to restrain Beau.

The heavy-lidded matron frowned at the wriggling cub. "I see. Well, it seems to me that you should have him professionally trained. You don't seem to be having any luck at all. He is quite unruly."

Wyeth stepped forward, clucking at Colin. "How true, Mrs. Castleman, how very true. I have tried to tell Colin that very thing. Colin, I said, get that dog professionally trained. If I've said it once, I've said it a hundred times, but . . ." Wyeth shrugged, rolling her eyes. "You know how stubborn men are." Wyeth sighed at the nodding woman who left them muttering "stubborn" to herself.

Wyeth held herself in control, keeping her face frozen until the elevator closed on Mrs. Castleman's rigid features. Then she gave a hoot of laughter that swiveled Colin's head from the dog toward her. The emerald green eyes had a determined glitter to them.

"I owe you for that one, Wyeth. I always pay my debts," he warned, amusement not quite masking his ire. "Let's get him to your suite."

Beau lunged again making Colin curse. "I should have put a choke collar on him. I know Albert has some that we used for the sled dogs we had years ago. Stop laughing at that fool pup, and let's get him to your rooms."

They were both panting by the time they reached the door, Colin finally carrying the dog. "Whew! Come inside, Wyeth. I'll close the door."

Wyeth barely heard Colin. She was too busy gazing at her new suite of apricot and cream, accented with azure blue. The sitting room was much larger than her other one had been, with a sunken conversation pit in front of a cream-colored brick fireplace. A three-sided apricot couch faced the fireplace. The ceiling was vaulted and beamed in logs. Behind the fireplace wall was the master bedroom of the two-bedroom suite with the fireplace opening into it as well.

Wyeth roamed through the apartment to the tiny chrome and black kitchen. Then she went into the bedroom and gasped at the circular bed covered with an apricot and cream silk quilt. She delighted in the dressing room between the bathroom and the bedroom, fitted with walls of drawers, a vanity, and a lighted walk-in closet that looked like a room itself. Her things looked lost there, neither filling the closet or the drawers. Wyeth reddened when she saw the sauna in the bathroom, remembering the moments that she and Colin had spent in the other one. She gritted her teeth when she heard him chuckle behind her and knew he had read her mind. Ignoring him, she pretended interest in the kidney-shaped tub with the two steps leading down into it. There was a separate shower stall with a convex sliding door in apricot glaze.

"Do you like it?" he breathed at her ear.

"Yes, of course I do," she answered, not looking at him when she slid past and returned to the bedroom.

"Where are you going in such a rush, Wyeth?" Colin queried, his husky voice making her pause in the doorway.

"I'm sure Beau is getting into some mischief. I don't relish him doing something awful to those Kirman rugs out there," she choked, hoping he wouldn't follow her as she searched for the dog.

"I thought maybe you were running from me because we were in the bedroom together," Colin said, extracting a cheroot from his pocket and lighting it.

"And I thought you never had more than one of those a day. That makes three," Wyeth replied, wishing she had the strength to toss him out the door.

He studied the lighted cigar for long moments. "You have a strange effect on me, Wyeth. Not good, it would seem. I intend to change everything to my satisfaction."

Wyeth felt the menace and took a step backward. "As you have pointed out to me several times, I should be in bed. So I'll say good night." She knew her voice was cold, but she didn't care. For a moment she thought he was going to balk, then with another assessing look he turned and left the suite. Wyeth gave a sigh of relief.

"Come along, dog. I'm going to bed you down in the bathroom."

When Wyeth woke to Beau's whining, it was four o'clock in the morning, but after she let him out onto the terrace for a few moments, he was happy to go back to his snug bed of towels in the bathroom.

The next time Wyeth woke up, Marie was tapping at the door, saying that she had Madame's coffee. As Wyeth struggled to a sitting position and told the young woman to enter, a long mournful howl came from the bathroom.

Marie heard it and frowned toward the sound. "Is that the wolf cub that Albert has told me about, madame?"

"Yes, Marie, I'm afraid it is. Don't you like dogs?" Wyeth inquired, trying not to laugh at the other's displeasure.

"Of a surety, I do, madame, but not at Montbel. Dogs are for the out-of-doors, madame. Shall I let him out of there?" she asked, setting the tray across Wyeth's knees and looking askance at the dressing-room door.

"Yes, please, he probably needs to go outside again. I can do that," Wyeth placated.

Marie took a deep sigh and lifted her hand, her palm facing Wyeth. "No, madame, I will do it. I am to care for you, and even if I do not approve of such nonsense, I will care for the dog as well. It is, of course, stupid, but I will do it."

Wyeth clutched at her mouth as the long suffering Marie let the dog free. Admonishing it in her high-pitched French, Marie tried to keep the dog in order, but the loose-limbed Beau slipped around her and galloped toward Wyeth, sailing onto the bed in one ungainly leap.

Marie shrieked, trying to tackle the animal, as Wyeth lifted her tray, trying to keep it from the reach of the dog's paws.

Beau thought it was a game so he crossed the bed, jumped off, then ran around onto the other side, leaped on again, and slid across Wyeth while Marie screamed and chased him.

"Wait, Marie, don't chase him. . . . Beau, stop that. Sit." Wyeth tried to shift out of the bed carrying the tray but couldn't budge because the charging dog was everywhere.

"What the hell is going on here?" Colin barked, fending off the dog as it jumped for him, and making the cub heel. "Marie, take that tray from Madame. We'll have our breakfast in the solarium." He turned back to the dog, speaking to it in very stern tones, then he let it outside. When he closed the sliding doors and looked at a shivering Wyeth under the bedclothes, he gave her

68

a hard look. "Don't worry about Beau; Albert is outside and is going to take him for a run. Shall I get your robe?"

"No, thank you. As soon as you leave, I'll get it myself," Wyeth stated, keeping the sheets under her chin so that he wouldn't know she was sleeping nude.

He turned to the door and paused. Without facing her he spoke again. "Don't worry, *petite*. I have seen the female form many times. Yours would be no novelty. I, too, sleep in the altogether. How nice to find we have one thing in common." He left shutting the door.

The pillow Wyeth threw almost reached the door. She catapulted from the bed, muttering to herself, kicking at the fallen pillow, slamming the bathroom door with force. "Who invited him for breakfast?" she asked the mirror image whose mouth was lathered in toothpaste.

What plans was he formulating? Wyeth asked herself as she stepped into jeans and a bulky knit burgundy turtleneck. She pulled on a pair of tan leather boots that gave her a long, leggy look.

With a feeling of déjà vu she opened the door to the front room. Colin rose from the couch in the conversation pit, his green eyes assessing as she walked toward him. Without speaking he gestured toward the solarium. Before she could pour the coffee from the pewter pot, his hand was there, filling her cup, amusement tingeing his lips when he saw her stiffen.

"Let me pour for you today, Wyeth. Are you angry that I make myself too much at home in your suite?" he queried, his drawl telling her that he didn't give a damn what she thought.

"Why should I mind? This was your suite after all," she said, her voice taut. "I really wish you had left me where I was—"

"What about Beau? You couldn't keep him upstairs with the other guests, could you?" he interrupted.

"No, but perhaps I could—" Wyeth began, picking her words.

"No buts, Wyeth. You stay here," he stated, brooking no argument.

"You're an arrogant cur, do you know that?" Wyeth sputtered. "Maybe the rest of the people here in Montbel don't mind your overbearing ways, but I won't be dictated to. You had better understand that."

"My, my, you're going to be a terror when you're fully recovered, aren't you?" Colin said low, taking a sip of his black French coffee and ambling to the suite door to let Marie in. He gestured with his head, and she set out a round table in the solarium. With deft motions Marie set the table with steaming foods and withdrew without speaking.

"Wyeth, come and have your juice. Here, take these tablets with them. Émile has prescribed a vitamin therapy for you." Colin ushered her into her chair, then poured five tablets into her hand from a small silver pillbox. Colin frowned when she hesitated, then he put a glass of iced orange juice into her hand.

"What do you do when you're not bullying people?" she asked, her voice cold. She glared at him when she coughed, trying to take all the vitamins at once, irritated at his amusement.

"Sometimes I work. I should be doing it now," he said, his lazy eyes sifting her brain as she watched him. For a panicky moment she had the feeling that he had, in truth, dissected her mind.

"Don't let me stop you." She jabbed at a piece of French toast, golden and crisp.

"Ah, such delightful manners. I feel so wanted," he gibed, saluting her with his tomato juice.

"Let me enjoy my breakfast, would you. I'll trade quips with you after I've digested my food." She smiled, her mouth closing over a piece of toast.

"Now that your mouth is full, Auntie dear, maybe I can say something." Colin smiled at her glare. "There's a board meeting this Tuesday. As a large shareholder, you can attend. That has been our policy in the past, since most of the shares are held by family."

"And I suppose you're chairman of the board." Wyeth swallowed the food in her mouth.

"You suppose right. If you prefer, I can vote your stock as I used to do for Nate, but—"

"I'll be there," Wyeth affirmed, looking him in the eye.

"I was sure you would say that," Colin replied, lifting his napkin to his mouth and leaning back in his chair, his eyes pinning her. He reached into his pocket and pulled the silver cigar case from its place.

She looked from the case to his eyes and smiled devilishly.

"No—don't say it," he warned. "Since your arrival I'm smoking more. Next I'll be drinking more," he drawled, his eyes green marble. "You have a bad effect on me, *petite.*"

"*Quelle surprise!* I didn't know anything bothered you," Wyeth mocked in a French accent.

His eyes narrowed. "Was that an imitation of Amalie?" Wyeth could tell his brain had shifted into high gear. "Amalie is a sensuous creature who revels in males but is bored by her own sex. Don't let her intimidate you, *chérie.* She doubly despises beautiful women."

Wyeth was glad when he looked down to light his slim black cigar. She didn't want him to see the red that she knew was staining her cheeks at his casual compliment. She broke the feather-light French toast into tiny pieces on her plate.

"What have you planned for the day, *petite*? There is much to do, but Émile tells me that he would rather you didn't push yourself too hard at first." Colin twirled the lighted cigar in his fingers.

"Don't worry about me. I thought I would go down to the library and find something to read. I want to stay with Beau for the first few days until he gets used to his home."

"And do you consider Montbel your home, Wyeth?" His eyes swung to her like twin green lasers.

Wyeth stiffened, unable to read that gaze. "How could I? After only three days here?"

"Has it been only three days, *ma mie*?" The green fire in his eyes washed over her—warmed her wherever his gaze touched. "Somehow it's seemed so much longer to me."

Colin uncoiled his length and stretched. "I have to leave you. I have paperwork this morning that won't wait."

Wyeth rose too but kept the table between them. She knew he noticed by the rough smile he wore as he turned to the door. She followed him, careful to keep a good distance behind him.

"Thank you for having breakfast with me." She cleared her throat wishing he would leave.

He whirled around before she could react and pulled her into his arms, bending his head to explore the hollows of her neck with his warm, wet mouth, paying no heed to her protests, propelling her even tighter into his hold.

The urgent pressure of his lips provoked hers open, and even as she chided her stupidity, her arms were raising to grasp him around the shoulders, her fingers twining in the thick springy hair at the nape of his neck.

CHAPTER FOUR

Wyeth struggled into the navy blue knickers, then pulled a white sweater over her head with an explosive sigh. "Are you sure this is how I'm supposed to look, Marie? My goodness, the clothing seems quite light for skiing . . ."

Marie giggled, her hand to her mouth. "Truly you are dressed right, Madame MacLendon. In fact, you will find yourself becoming most warm . . . but . . . you must not remove your clothing. Albert will instruct you how you are to go on, madame . . ." Marie paused to rescue Wyeth's glove from Beau, who was happily worrying it. "I think you most unwise to take this thankless creature with you. . . . Stop that, naughty one. *Mon Dieu!* He will eat your entire wardrobe, to be sure."

Wyeth laughed and grasped the leash that Albert had sent for Beau, pulling the dog toward the door while she clucked encouragement to him.

"What shall I tell Monsieur Colin when he asks where you are, madame? I am sure if you could wait for the afternoon, he would take you skiing himself . . ." Marie forestalled her in an anxious voice.

"Not to worry, Marie, really. Colin won't be worried about me. Just tell him I'm skiing and will be back in . . . well . . . an hour . . ." Wyeth said not looking at Marie, her words more confident than her thoughts. She wondered what the young woman would think if Wyeth told her that she was trying to avoid seeing Colin . . . that she couldn't think in his company.

Somehow she had to get away from him and marshal her thoughts. The man was the most arrogant, irritating person she had ever met. She despised him. Even more, she despised herself for the woolly feeling she had in his presence. It annoyed her that her logical mind became goo when she talked to him. Macho boor, she grated to herself.

Breaking free of the fretting Marie, who seemed to need assurance that she was strong enough for the Quebec winters, was not easy.

"Marie, I've been resting for three weeks. I'm strong as a horse, and like a horse, I'm itching for a run. Honestly, I'm fine, and I've done a great deal of downhill skiing, so don't worry." Wyeth escaped before the maid could answer her, pulling the dog with her as she scampered down the stairway leading to the basement level and along the corridor to the ski shop. She grinned in answer to Albert's slow smile as he watched her with the frisky animal. "You're right, Albert. He does eat like a pig."

"He is big, that one, madame. I think he has gained fifty pounds."

Wyeth laughed and agreed. "Are the skis ready, Albert? Oh yes, I see them. Now, if you will just give me some instructions—"

"Madame, I think it is better that you wait for Monsieur Colin or one of the others to accompany you. Monsieur Colin is very good with the skis." Albert nodded, his pipe stabbing the air.

Wyeth gave him her most winning smile, not able to explain even to herself why she just couldn't have Monsieur Colin with her. "I have the map, Albert, and I don't intend to go far. Where is that infernal map? Ah, here it is. See! Now, show me please."

In short order Albert gave her the rudiments on how to manage herself in cross-country skiing. Wyeth felt she could handle the beginners' trail despite Albert's objections. She was sure that Beau would follow along with her, but just in case, she had tucked his leash into her pocket. As she fitted the ski bindings

74

tighter she marveled at the ease of movement afforded by the gear.

"Come on, Beau. 'Bye, Albert." She whistled to the dog and pushed off, shaky at first but gaining confidence with every forward thrust of the skis.

"Come on, Beau." Her breath puffed out in front of her. "Albert says we are to take the trail at the front of the château, and it will lead us to the flagged trails." Muttering the instructions Albert had given to her and calling to Beau took much of her concentration. She had stuffed the map, an extra pair of gloves, and a Thermos into her backpack, along with two apples and a box of crackers. Her hands were free to maneuver the poles. She skimmed along without too much wobbling.

When she came to the fork in the trail that began the flagged trails, she tried to remember what Albert had told her about them. It was easier to try and remember than to unload her backpack and read the map. "Let me think. Did he say red was for beginners or advanced? I know blue is for intermediate. Beau, you should have listened." Wyeth laughed at the cub tearing through the snow in big circles.

"Oh, well, I'm sure orange is for beginners." Shrugging, she dug in her poles and took the left-hand trail. At first it was quite open. Wyeth remembered the golf course that was on the map. Then the trail took a steep turn downward. Wyeth tried to snowplow but found it more difficult with the loose boot. She felt herself picking up speed. Remembering what Albert said about losing control, she sat down in the snow and slid for some feet on her bottom. She sat there laughing at Beau who thought it was a game to play. He at once began to lick her face.

"Stop it, Beau, I won't be able to get up with you jumping on me like that. My, isn't it quiet! I must say I have far more respect for this sport after seeing this beginner trail. Lord, Beau, don't cock your head at me like that. Do I seem crazy to you because I talk to you so much? Enough of this; let me up . . ."

It took Wyeth four sweating, puffing tries before she made it to her feet. The trail was both narrow and steep, causing her no end of difficulties. She fell twice more on the way down the curving grade before she managed a sloppy plow near the bottom. She crossed a snow-covered road and for about a hundred feet she was in open ground again, then she entered a hilly wooded area that took all her concentration and skill as a downhiller to handle. She kept her eyes down, only checking for the orange flags and Beau, who kept pace with her easily and never seemed to tire.

The sun was high above them when Wyeth called a halt to eat her crackers and drink from her Thermos. She was hot and perspiring freely, glad to remove her gloves and rub some of the cold snow on her face. She felt as though her entire body were the color of a tomato.

"Here, Beau, have a cracker. Oh, don't be so greedy. You can hardly have tasted that. How far do you think we've gone, boy? Beau, did anyone ever tell you that you're a very restful companion. Come on, it's time to move . . ."

Wyeth took pride in the fact that she was moving so effortlessly now, but as the afternoon moved along, she found herself tiring. She paused at one point to remove her map from her backpack and study it.

"The way I see it, Beau, we're almost at the point of no return . . . so . . . we'll go forward and follow the trail all the way around to the junction. I hope this half will be easier than the first . . ." Wyeth rambled on to Beau, the map clutched in one mittened fist. The second perusal of the map made her give a gasp. "Oh, Lord, Beau, we're on the expert run. The red flag marks the beginner run, and we're on the orange. No wonder I'm having such a rough time . . ." She sighed, digging in her poles and whistling to the dog. Wyeth figured she might as well continue onward rather than turn back. The trail behind her had been tough. She had to hope that ahead of her was easier.

Wyeth was sorry she hadn't turned back after about thirty minutes of executing tortuous turns and twists. She fell down innumerable times, just bruising her dignity rather than her limbs. She gritted her teeth and pushed on. She stopped a few times to rest but didn't feel the nerve-crushing fatigue she had suffered in times past. There were no doubts in her mind about her ability to make it back to *Le Château.*

After a heart-bursting climb up a narrow trail, she and Beau arrived at the top of a tiny ridge. Wyeth could feel her mouth dropping open as she looked down the serpentine ski way.

"My God, Beau, it looks like a bobsled run. Perhaps I should walk down. . . . No, I won't do that. We shall ski down, Beau . . . well, I mean, I will. You stay near me, and pick up the pieces." Wyeth grinned down at the tail-wagging animal with his tongue hanging from the side of his mouth. "Here we go, boy; stay clear of me . . ."

Wyeth pushed off gently, her skis in snowplow position. At once she felt the skid of ice, and panic feathered her spine. Gritting her teeth, she dug in her poles, and through the sides of her boots she felt the skis slide around the first downward turn. She choked as the tree-lined tunnel took a drastic forty-five degree drop. She managed to keep control, but her speed had picked up alarmingly. The wind whistled against her cheek as she tried to check her momentum. She whirled around another bend and felt a tree limb tear at her sweater. Just when she thought she was going to make it, within the last fifty yards her pole caught in a bush, throwing her off balance for a second. It was enough. Before she could recover, she felt her left ski go sideways. Wyeth heard the crack of the ski as it hit a tree; then she was falling, tumbling down the narrow slope. She let herself relax fully as she had been taught in downhill. There was a wrench in her body, then the skis released, her poles went flying, and she kept rolling, finally to come to rest against some scrub.

She lay for a moment, dazed, then Beau was at her side, licking her face. She pushed him away, gingerly checking to see if all was as right as it felt.

"All right, Beau, all right. I just have a few bruises, thank goodness. Now let's go back up there and find my skis and poles . . ."

She was feeling rather good about the whole thing until she picked up her left ski. It had splintered from the point almost back to the fitting. Wyeth grimaced as she remembered the sound of the ski hitting the tree.

It had started to snow. Wyeth grimaced at the lacy flakes descending in slow motion all around her. Beau snapped at the snow, taken aback when the snowflake turned to water in his mouth. "You fool." Wyeth laughed at the puzzled dog. "You may end up carting me out of here." She stared up at the sun, now almost obscured by the falling snow. "It's close to noon. We've been out here for about four hours," Wyeth mused out loud, feeling sudden fatigue. Giving herself a mental shake, she stuck her broken ski upright in the snow, collected her poles, and put them over one shoulder with the one good ski. It would have been easier to leave both skis, but Wyeth reasoned that she might find a use for the one good ski.

Trudging down the steep, curving trails was easier because her boots sank in the snow and kept her from slipping, but it was hard work. She could feel the perspiration between her shoulders. At the same time she felt the cold more than she had when she had been moving along on skis. She tried to keep the orange flags in sight, but as the snow thickened, she was more inclined to keep her head down and trudge along behind the easily moving Beau.

They had traveled a mile or more when Wyeth decided it had been too long since she had seen an orange flag. She stopped, lifting her burden from her shoulder and propping it against a tree, and eased the backpack from her body with a sigh. She straightened to look through the falling snow but could see no orange flag. Panic laced her for a moment as she recalled just how expansive the territory was. "The seigneury is over a hundred square miles" she could hear Mr. Wingate saying.

She leaned down to pat the panting Beau. "I think we have

78

got off the marked trail, dog. I think while we can still see, we had better retrace our steps." Wyeth could hear the tiredness in her voice. She bit her lip. "I won't give in to this," she muttered, setting the other ski into the snow with a downward thrust. "C'mon, dog, back we go. I wish it would stop snowing. It's beginning to fill in our steps already."

Each step was becoming a chore, but Wyeth pushed on, watching for the orange flags. Wyeth glanced at her watch and realized that more time had passed than she had figured. She looked around her, and with a stab of fear realized that she had taken another turnoff and had not gone back to the original trail. With a sobbing sigh she leaned against a tree, shivering, slapping her hands together, and trying to keep her feet moving. Beau sat in front of her, staring at her.

When she heard the low howl, she didn't pay attention until she saw Beau turn, the hackles on his back raising, his lip curling back from his teeth in a snarl.

Wyeth was wide-awake, peering into the thick curtain of snow, her one hand going down to Beau's back. "What is it, boy? I hope it isn't any of your relatives seeking us out," she whispered to the quivering animal. As though he could sense her trepidation, Beau backed closer to her, his stance stiff-legged and aware. Not once did he turn to look at her but kept his eyes dead in front of him.

The howl came again, closer this time. Wyeth took a grip on the poles and wished she had kept the one ski with her. She started to shake with cold.

The crack of rifle fire made Wyeth cry out in alarm. Beau let out a combination yelp and howl.

"Beau. Beau." The yell came. Then there was another shot, much nearer. Beau yelped again, his tail swinging in slow cadence.

"We're here. We're here, Colin," Wyeth sobbed, recognizing his voice at once. She slid down the tree trunk to huddle, cold but relieved, against the frozen bark.

He burst through the curtain of snow like a black wraith, setting Beau into a frenzy of yelping and howling as the dog jumped all over him. "All right. Easy now, boy. Good dog." Colin patted the dog but looked at Wyeth, placing his rifle against a tree and stripping the gloves from his hands to get the flask from his inner pocket. "What the hell were you trying to do? Set an endurance record? You know damn well you shouldn't have come out here alone. Here, swallow some of this. Can you hold it? Good. I have to fire the signal that you're safe. The whole patrol is out looking for you," Colin rasped, the words coming like bullets from his mouth, as his hand ran through his beard. He slung the rifle up and fired three shots in rapid succession. "All right, we're getting out of here. I found your broken ski and your other one." He looked at her in hard-eyed appraisal as she stood. "I have other skis here. Can you make it or should I go for the travois?"

"I can ski if it's not too far . . . but I'm cold." Wyeth spoke through stiff lips.

"It's zero degrees and snowing, so that's natural. Let's go. It's not too far from here," he rasped, fitting the skis on her and urging her forward.

They stopped several times while Colin fed her hot sweet tea from the Thermos and gulps of brandy from the flask. Wyeth was beginning to feel decidedly light-headed as she reeled down the trail after Colin, the devoted Beau at her side.

When she looked up to see why they had stopped, she didn't even have the strength to question where they were. She knew it wasn't the château, but she had a hazy glimpse of a chalet-type building built with the usual logs. The gingerbread at the front was outlined in vivid red, contrasting sharply with the dark-hued logs. Then Colin was releasing her fastenings and lifting her into his arms. The sudden warmth of the interior of the building was almost too much for her dazed state. She made no demur when Colin carried her up the stairs, wide-open to the rest of the downstairs, along an open balcony to a bedroom that was paneled in oak, with an oak floor scattered with Oriental rugs. Her glazed eyes took note of the king-size bed covered with a silken quilt in blue. Then they were in a bathroom, and Colin was holding her with one hand while he fiddled with the fixtures in the sunken tub. Water swirled into the round tub, steam rising in welcome clouds. Wyeth said nothing as he stripped her clothes, tested the water, then lifted her down into the soothing depths. Her skin tingled in painful wakening as the cold receded from her body. She slid down into the depths, not caring if she drowned. She smelled a fragrance and realized that Colin had added something to the water.

"This is not just for beauty uses, Wyeth. These salts I'm adding will soothe your skin and your nerves. I buy this from an Indian friend of mine. His grandfather is a great medicine man, and he makes up this bath essence for me, plus other mixes of herbs that are salutary to the body and spirit," Colin drawled, putting his hand on her cheek.

"How delightful for your girl friends: special bath oils to relax them. My, my, you certainly think of everything." Wyeth tried in vain to stem the series of yawns that overtook her. "But then again, I suppose you do a lot of . . . entertaining."

"Usually my women don't fall asleep on me," Colin chuckled.

"I'm not one of your women," Wyeth murmured, opening one eye. "So don't forget it." She felt her body slide further into the froth. Then Colin was washing her body with a Loofa sponge, stroking life back into her aching limbs. She tried to tell him to stop, that she could wash herself, but it was too much trouble to speak. She felt herself lifted from the water after a time, her head nestled against his soft beard, then her body was wrapped in a fluffy towel that had been heated. She felt her head swing back and forth as Colin dried her hair and realized that he had shampooed her as well as bathed her. Sleep cocooned her before she felt the mattress at her back, the quilt cuddling her naked body.

* * *

She didn't want to waken, but something was pulling her to a conscious state as hard as she fought against it. Coffee. She smelled coffee, and bacon. She sniffed in avid appreciation. There was toast. She slid upward on the bed, wishing Marie would bring her breakfast, when all at once she realized she was in a strange bed.

The previous day flooded over her. Colin had brought her to a strange house. She had slept here all night! Open-mouthed, she looked out the floor-to-ceiling windows to the sun being refracted off the snow. Whose house was this? she asked herself, as she swung her legs out of the bed. She was sitting there, uncovered, when Colin pushed open the door and walked in carrying a tray, Beau at his side.

The dog made to leap for her, but a sharply spoken word from Colin restrained him, so that he only wriggled in delight at her feet as Wyeth tried to pull the blue quilt around her.

Colin set the tray on the dresser and turned to her, studying her as though she were a test that he would have to pass. "I'll get you something to cover you while we eat." He made no effort to leave but walked toward her, bending down to press his lips against her bare shoulder. "Would you like to eat in bed, or shall I set it on the table in front of the window?" he breathed into her ear.

"Yes."

"Yes, what?" Colin answered, his lips on her cheek, amusement in his voice.

"Yes, near the window." Wyeth pushed back from him, gnashing her teeth when he let his eyes rove over her again. "May I have the covering please, or at least don't lean on the quilt so that I can use that."

He whirled with a grin and entered what Wyeth assumed was a dressing room. He was back in a moment with a short toweling robe, which he draped across her back. It was much too long in the arms, and he folded the sleeves back for her. "Shall I carry you?" he whispered.

82

"No, I can walk," she said, rising, then falling back down to the bed. "Well, perhaps I'll take your arm, but I want to walk. Why am I weak?"

"The aftermath of exposure. Émile says you are to stay here for a few days and recuperate." He grinned at her glare. "It wasn't my idea, but even so, I think we would have had to stay anyway. It's still snowing. We could only get out of here on a snowmobile, and Émile agrees with me that you are not up to such a trip yet. You are marooned with me, *Tante*. I have you at my mercy." He leered.

"Not bloody likely," Wyeth snapped, glad to sink into the chair he held for her, surprised at how far it was from the bed to the little nook in front of the windows. She looked down at the browned slices of bacon and the fluffy omelet and raised her brows at him in question.

"Yes, I can cook. I can also nurse foolish ladies who lose themselves in the snow."

"What a paragon! I'm surprised you haven't been snapped up," Wyeth crooned.

"Nasty little scold!" Colin drawled. "Not even a thank you for saving your delightful hide?"

Anger and shame battled within her. Shame won. "I am grateful to you and to all the other persons who came looking for me. I hope you will tell me who they are, so that I can thank them personally."

"I'll tell you if you promise not to tear into them the way you do to me." Colin munched on a piece of toast, an expectant gleam in his green eyes.

"You know damn well that you provoke me constantly," Wyeth lashed, then pulled back when she saw him put back his head and laugh. She gasped. "You did that on purpose."

"Yes, which proves my point that you're a shrew," he remarked, leaning back in his chair, balancing it on two legs.

Stung, Wyeth glared at him, not wanting him to know how much his criticism hurt. "Until I met you, I was known for my even-tempered nature, I would like you to know," she informed him, stiff-lipped.

"Bull."

"I am tempted to upend that silver coffeepot on your head," Wyeth informed him through her teeth. "But I'm sure someone as thick-skinned as you wouldn't even notice."

"Wrong. If you did that, weak or not, I'd turn you back out in the snow."

"And I'd walk back to Montbel—even in this ridiculous robe!" she shot back, unable to analyze the ripple of feeling that coursed through her while he was staring at her.

Colin rose to his feet. Wyeth felt dwarfed when he stretched his hands high over his head and yawned. "Finish your juice. You're going back to bed, and so am I."

"Not in that bed, you're not." She stamped a bare foot on the Oriental rug.

His arms came down as he gave her a weary smile. "No, Auntie, not in your bed. I couldn't take the abuse at this point. I didn't get much sleep last night. I need it now."

"You were foolish to sit up watching over me," she answered tartly, feeling remorse at the thought of him being up all night.

"I wasn't watching over you. I was sleeping on a cot in the dressing room, and it was damned uncomfortable. I don't know why the hell they make those things so short." He yawned again.

"You're too tall. That's the trouble." Wyeth tried not to lean on him as he led her back to the bed, a now sleeping Beau snoring in the corner.

He nodded, blinking his eyes as she slid into the bed. "I should have known you would think it's my fault. Here. Give me the robe."

"I'll remove it after you're gone." She spoke firmly, her hands crossed on her arms, sitting straight on the bed, never taking her eyes from him.

"Suit yourself." He yawned, turning from her to lift the tray from the table, then walk from the room without another word.

Wyeth let her body slide on the silken sheets. She still felt groggy, so she lay back, sighing in comfort.

She was beginning to doze when the phone rang next to her bed. She let it ring a few times, thinking maybe Colin would answer it. On the fourth ring she picked up the receiver. "Hello?"

"Well, well, you do seem better," Amalie crooned. "I thought by the description that Émile gave me that you were at death's door."

"I doubt if Dr. Tiant would exaggerate so," Wyeth answered in clipped tones, angry that the woman would call here, yet unable to see why she should be angry.

"Let me speak to Colin," Amalie demanded, her voice no longer soft.

"I'm sorry, I can't. He was up all night and needs his sleep." Wyeth took malicious satisfaction in hearing Amalie's gasp of rage. Before the other woman could say more Wyeth broke the connection, then lifted the receiver from the hook and left it on the table. When the warning buzzer hummed over the wire, Wyeth glared at it. "Well, it's true. He does need his sleep. He said so himself."

She swung her feet out of bed and sat up, deciding she would look over the house. She liked what she had seen, finding its looks deceiving. From the outside it had given no clue to its airy spaciousness. She showered and dressed in record time, grimacing at her wrinkled clothing. She felt uncomfortable but shrugged the feeling away since there was nothing that she could do.

She walked out into the corridor that was open to the common room one floor down and thought how much the chalet repeated the style of Montbel. She studied the gingerbready ceiling all done in oak and marveled at the way it was picked out in red like the outside. She walked down the suspended stairway that was just two-by-twelves of plank oak and ambled toward the kitchen that was separated from the common room by a bar with stools on both sides. The kitchen had a work island in the center, and the walls were all cupboards except for the sliding-glass doors that led to a deck in the shape of a ship's prow. More sliding doors led onto the deck from the bow-shaped eating area that was open to the kitchen and the common room, and held a large oaken table with eight carved oak chairs. Heriz Orientals were everywhere but the kitchen, which had a slate floor. The vivid blues and reds of the Orientals were compatible with the deep brown of the oak. The fireplace in the common room was of stone and reached the ceiling: the tingeing of black on the stones told of its use, but also that someone had worked hard to keep the blacking from coloring the stone.

Wyeth wondered who cleaned the place; she also wondered who owned it. She knew it must belong to a friend of Colin's or Colin himself because he had shown himself to be very familiar with the place. Mardi and Kyle had told her that Colin had a nice place, she mused, one hand pushing at her curls; maybe this was the one.

She strolled toward the sliding-glass doors leading to the front deck. That, too, was in the shape of the prow of a ship. The snow was falling like feathers from a shaken pillow. The wind during the night had swept the snow halfway up the door, acting like a soundproofing. There was no sound or movement in that white expanse, dotted here and there with evergreens. The visibility was poor, but the gray silhouette of Montbel pierced the gloom, its peaks obscured in the clouds of snow. Wyeth had no idea in what direction the château would be or how far it would be.

"Does it give you a lonely feeling, Wyeth?" Colin's voice startled her, swinging her around to face him. He was dressed in a toweling sarong, his chestnut hair now darkened to black by wetness. He moved with easy grace over to the fireplace and put a match to the bed of logs and paper. In a few moments orange tongues were leaping up the chimney. He turned back to her, one eyebrow raised as though waiting for her to answer his question.

"No, it doesn't make me feel lonely. It has a barren beauty that pulls you, I think. I am surprised by the amount of snow you have."

"We've had one hundred and forty inches already this year, *petite.*" He smiled as Wyeth's eyes widened. "Or, perhaps you enjoy feeling isolated, eh?"

Wyeth shook her head, watching him.

"Is that why you left the phone off the hook?" Colin quizzed, lowering himself onto the couch and stretching his long bare legs in front of him.

Wyeth's face burned. "I did it because I thought you wanted to sleep." After all, that was true, she thought. "All you have to do is replace the receiver."

"I did." He leaned back, giving a contented grunt as he stroked his beard. "I needed a vacation. Being snowed in won't be an inconvenience to me. What about you, Wyeth?"

"It doesn't bother me." She dissembled. "Surely they'll try to get through from Montbel. You told me you're a busy man."

He shrugged. "I am, but my brother is learning the business and doing well. This is a good opportunity for him."

"What about the stockholders' meeting? You must want to be there."

"I do," he rasped, not elaborating, his mouth tightening. For long moments there was silence. Wyeth wandered around the room feeling gauche as a schoolgirl and hating her awkwardness. "Are you going to tell me who called before?" His voice was low, but Wyeth stiffened as though he shouted at her.

"It was Amalie. She wanted to talk to you. I told her you were sleeping. I think she worries about you." Wyeth finished, her smile steady.

"Does she?" Colin quizzed, his smile as bland as hers. "Why do I get the feeling you don't like Amalie?"

"I couldn't guess where your ideas come from," Wyeth spoke, her voice bored. "I wouldn't care to speculate about the state of your mind at any time."

"You've a sharp tongue, haven't you, Auntie?" Colin laughed.

"Only when I'm unduly provoked, Nephew," Wyeth snapped, not liking the direction the conversation was taking. She turned toward the door.

"Want to help me pick the wine we'll be having for dinner?"

She spoke without turning around. "It's a little early in the day, isn't it?"

"I said we'd choose it, not drink it. It's not that early, though." He flashed a look at the chased gold watch on his wrist. "It's after two." He smiled as her mouth dropped open, her eyes turning to the grandfather clock standing near the front door, just as it began to chime the hour. "You were worn out, Wyeth. You didn't waken until noon."

"I must have been tired, but I feel rested now."

"Good. Come and help me choose the wine. I want you to see the cellar." He stretched his hand toward her, and she clasped it at once.

"Don't you think you should dress first?"

"Does my appearance offend you?" His brows rose. "You've seen me in less," he taunted.

She could feel color rising in her cheeks. "I only thought that a wine cellar would be on the cool side," she said tartly.

"I'll risk it." He grinned at her, holding a door open under the floating staircase.

A wide set of stairs led down into a darkened interior, which Colin lighted from a switch near the door. They descended side by side into the stone-walled room lined with shelves much like a library, but instead of books there were bottles. Not all the shelves were filled—but enough of them to let Wyeth know that Colin was a collector, of sorts.

"A slight hobby." He answered her quizzical look. "I say 'slight' because I'm not in the class my father or grandfather were, but I do put up a few bottles if I like the vintage." He hadn't released her hand, and now he led her down the rows explaining in simple terms what the bottles were.

"We're having chicken with truffles tonight, so tell me what

88

you'd like," Colin invited, leading her toward some wines, naming them and telling her about the contents of the bottles.

Wyeth finally chose a Pouilly-Fuissé and felt warmth run through her when Colin applauded her choice.

Colin insisted that she was to sit in the kitchen and supervise while he put the meal together. He finally allowed her to chop the eggs for the spinach salad they would have, watching as Colin made the vinaigrette himself.

"When I was a boy I worked in the kitchens of Montbel, as well as being a busboy while in college. I learned quite a bit in the kitchen, and Marie Clair, mother of our existing chef, had no hesitation in boxing my ears if something wasn't done to her satisfaction."

Wyeth laughed, clapping her hands together.

Colin was beside her in an instant, lifting her from the chair up against the Hoover apron he had tied about himself. "You're too happy about my having my ears boxed. I'll have to revenge myself."

Wyeth wriggled, sputtering at him to put her down.

Laughing, his mouth swooped, silencing her. She felt herself suspended in his arms as he held her tighter, her feet dangling. She struggled for short moments, then felt the kiss change. His mouth softened on hers, coaxing her, his beard tickling her lips. His one hand still held her, but the other came up to tease the tiny hollow behind her ear. She gasped against his mouth, and he moved to take the advantage, his tongue touching at her mouth, teasing her tongue, making her body start to melt against him like snow.

His mouth left hers to explore the sensitive cord in her neck. She could hear guttural sounds of satisfaction emanating from his throat. She fought to keep herself on keel as his one arm tightened and the other searching hand became more urgent.

"The chicken," she gasped.

"Damn the chicken," he muttered, his mouth sliding over her skin.

89

"I'm hungry." She tried to rally.

"So am I," he mumbled.

Wyeth turned to liquid at his words but forced herself to stiffen against him. "I'm hungry for food."

"Mundane creature, aren't you?" Colin hissed into her neck, his teeth nipping hard at her earlobe. He lowered her to the floor by inches, placing one last hard kiss on her lips before releasing her. He turned from her so fast that she staggered.

By the time she was breathing steadily, he was basting the wine sauce over the crisp golden chicken breasts that had been boned and stuffed with truffles and parsley, then rolled and sliced in rounds. The silence between them wasn't strained, but it would have been an effort to converse, so they avoided it.

They dined on the oval coffee table that lifted into a dining-table height when Colin pressed a lever underneath. Two Sheraton chairs were brought from the walls down into the conversation pit, and they dined with just the flickering fire for light. They had éclairs for dessert that Colin had defrosted from the freezer.

"Marie Clair still supervises the pastry making, and she always makes sure there is plenty in my freezer," Colin explained, filling her glass before she could demur. "We must finish the wine or throw it out."

When they finished, Wyeth insisted on carrying the dishes to the kitchen, knowing that even such slight exercise would clear her brain somewhat. Colin worked at her side filling the dishwasher, and Wyeth knew that he was watching her with those all-knowing eyes of his, summing up her condition, her responses, her reactions before she could ever know them herself. He was a very annoying individual.

She was wiping the counter when he turned her around, loosened the apron, wiped her hands dry, then threaded his own fingers through hers leading her from the kitchen.

Wyeth felt trapped. Every sense warned her to run. Every nerve ending quivered at the threat of him. "It was a wonderful meal. I probably should get some sleep."

"Of course, but you're well enough to listen to a little music. I have a very nice liqueur I'd like you to try. It will relax you. So will the music."

Her protest caught in her throat like a pit, making her feel breathless. As the music filled the room like a cocoon she accepted the minuscule crystal with the amber liquid in it.

"This is a liqueur made by the Montbel vignerons. We have vineyards on the Niagara Escarpment and take great pride in our wines. We think this tastes much like its counterpart that comes from France," Colin said, sinking down into the couch next to her, his one arm resting along the back of the couch. "What do you think?"

"I'm no connoisseur, of course, but it tastes like cognac to me." Wyeth cleared her throat, trying not to let him see that she was leaning away from him.

"Ah, an educated palate! You would please our vignerons." He twisted the glass so that the amber liquid caught the flickering gold light of the fire, refracting on the cut crystal like topazes. "Why do I get the feeling you are uneasy, Aunt?" Colin drawled, staring into her surprised eyes as her head whipped around. "Am I boring you?" he said, his tones silken, as his one hand lifted to touch the dampened curls on her forehead.

"Don't be ridiculous," she snapped, wanting to wipe the beads of moisture from her lip but not wanting him to see her do it.

"Good," he stated, lifting the glass from her hand, setting it on the table, and then pulling her into his arms. "Then, you won't mind if we sit and listen to the music in a more comfortable position."

"Comfortable for whom?" Wyeth squeaked, trying to wriggle free but desisting when she caught him grinning down at her. "I wasn't uncomfortable in my other position." Wyeth cleared her throat, forcing herself not to look away from those glittering eyes.

"Fine, then indulge me. I'm more comfortable this way." He

pulled her across him so that she was almost lying on him, his one arm around her shoulders, the other resting on her hip.

Stiff at first, Wyeth began relaxing as the beguiling piano concerto echoed around them. She allowed her head to rest under his chin, her half-closed eyes on the fire.

She didn't stir as his one hand stroked her tenderly from her waist down the length of her leg and back again. She sighed when she felt his lips on her hair, his hand tightening on her shoulder.

"You're a beautiful naiad, Wyeth," he murmured, his stroking hand in velvet cadence under her breast, his questing fingers making every nerve ending tingle and respond as though to a tuning fork.

With a choked protest Wyeth tried to rise, but his arms wouldn't release her. Instead they roved her body in a more searching way, one hand going to her chin to tip her head back against his shoulder. His lips closed her eyes, then feathered to her mouth. When she tried to speak, his mouth took hers in slow possession.

"Your body says you want me as much as I want you," he teased in soft tones.

"My body lies." Wyeth struggled like a drowning person, feeling her resistance ebb.

He chuckled against her mouth, his tongue coaxing her lips open. With one fierce movement he shifted her body beneath him, holding her face still between his hands and looking down into her eyes.

"No," she railed, trying to push him away. "You don't own me, Colin. I'm not here to satisfy your every wish."

"That's right, you're not." His smile was rueful, but he didn't look away from her. "If I'm not careful, I'll be the one in bondage."

"Don't flatter yourself. I wouldn't have you on a silver plate," she snapped, trying to rally her scattering wits.

"Good. Neither of us wants a tie. We both want each other.

92

Why deny it?" Colin's mouth curved upward as he punctuated each word with the touch of his lips on her face.

"I deny everything," Wyeth said weakly, her hands tugging at the hair at his nape, loving the springy feel that tingled at her fingertips.

"Coward," Colin growled, his hands easing the clothing from her body as he held her captive among the silken cushions.

She had a fleeting awareness of his expertise as he undressed her; then she was naked to his view. She couldn't tear her eyes from his face as those emerald eyes roamed over every inch of her, his hands touching as his gaze did. She wanted to please him, to make him want her more than he had ever wanted a woman.

"You're perfect." His eyes never left her breasts as his fingers teased the rose-pink tips. "For God's sake, Wyeth, tell me you want it as much as I do." His voice was hoarse as he bent over her, his mouth teasing her navel, roving over her body, making her mindless.

"Yes," she shouted; but it came out a croak, her hands straining at his neck, impatient with him now.

He swept her up into his arms and carried her to his bedroom, his hands caressing her body, his own shirt flapping open, his mouth still stroking her mouth.

He pushed her down into the cushions strewn over the bed, scattering his own clothes, his eyes never leaving hers. He was simply magnificent to look at, to touch—his long muscular legs and physique a perfect study of masculine beauty. Wyeth felt an urgent desire to be close to him, to feel his tawny, hair-roughened skin pressed against every inch of her.

His eyes were green velvet as he sank down next to her, folding her into his strong embrace, his voice husky. "Tell me again you want me, because I need you more than I have ever wanted or needed anything. Tell me," he urged, his mouth pressed between her breasts, his beard grazing her soft, sensitive skin.

Her affirmative answer inflamed him more. Wyeth could feel

his struggle for control as he brought her to the edge of fulfillment.

Their lovemaking was devastating to them both, shattering any preconceived notions about the act of love. Wyeth felt his body shudder against her own as he muttered her name over and over, the thrust of his body taking her to the brink of consciousness.

When Wyeth lay limp and gasping in his arms, Colin passed a gentle hand over her damp forehead. "*Petite,* you never cease to surprise me. I find my desire for you not lessened but increased," he muttered, trying to laugh.

Wyeth tried to rise but Colin stilled her movements, a question in his eyes. "I thought I'd go back to my own room."

"No, darling, we'll share this one. Now close your eyes before I decide that I haven't had enough," he rasped, his teeth grazing her neck.

Wyeth was sure she wouldn't be able to sleep wrapped as she was in Colin's arms. It surprised her to be woken later by Colin's mouth at her navel, his mutterings soothing if incomprehensible. She gave only a token struggle before she was submerged once more in the heady, cloudless planet of love. She was sure no woman had ever felt as she did, and then all thoughts disappeared. It shocked her when she realized that the purring sounds were coming from her own throat.

They hardly spoke, but the feeling of contentment was there. Sleep claimed them both again.

Morning was a slash of sunlight in a strange room. For long moments Wyeth tried to orient herself and ease away from the burden across her body. Colin had locked her to him with a hand on her breast and one leg entwined with hers. She looked into his sleeping face, amazed at what she had done. She never remembered feeling such a compulsion to love a man. With Harry it had been different. She had found their love play pleasant but not essential. She had reasoned that all her parents' adjurations on saving herself for marriage had colored their relationship, making her lukewarm about Harry's insistence that they share an apartment. With Colin she felt no such hesitation. She felt herself redden as she admitted that if he had held back, she could have become the aggressor. She shut her eyes, trying to wipe the thoughts from her mind.

No, she could not have refused Colin, not last night, not ever again. She looked at his face, the stern features gentled by sleep, and she recalled the green fire that had burned so brilliantly in his eyes last night. She suddenly imagined a life where Colin would always be beside her, gazing at her with those luminous green eyes. She knew that she had been drawn to him from the first, but now she realized that it was much more than attraction, more than desire. She had fallen in love with him. She would give her soul to be near him always, to have him look at her the way he had last night.

But what had last night meant to him? A physical appeasement, a mutual attraction brought to its logical conclusion, most likely. And then, too, there was her share of Montbel to be considered. Was this his way of taking full control, of binding her to him body and soul? If that had been his purpose, then he had succeeded, she thought sadly. He had succeeded more thoroughly than she would care to admit. Lord, how she wished she could trust him. But what woman in her right mind would dare?

"Good morning, darling." His mouth grazed her cheek, then her throat, his hand curling on her breast in a caress, the thumb rubbing her nipple erect. He chuckled at the instant arousal.

"I used to think that love songs and love stories were bull when they talked about 'people being made for each other.' I don't feel that way anymore, *petite*. We're made for each other." His voice was thick, making her aware that he wanted her again. "Your body was made for mine, wasn't it, darling?"

Before she had time to answer his mouth closed on hers, his whole body moving on hers with an urgency that set her on fire. She cried aloud as his mouth trailed over her from foot to chin, finding each pulse point, each tiny cave of sensation. When he finally covered her body with his, she clutched lovingly at his shoulders, all her dark suspicions forgotten, her tongue tasting the sweat on his cheeks.

The savage implosion shook her body. It gave her fierce satisfaction to feel his body shudder again and again with her. She felt one with him, this man she loved, flung out together to the farthest reaches of heaven.

Afterward he clasped her as tightly as she held him. In a despairing moment Wyeth fought the impulse to admit her love. She was glad that he wouldn't want to marry her though, she told herself. As his mistress she didn't really belong to him, nor he to her. Perhaps the jinx that Amalie was quick to mention would overlook such a nebulous union. It pained her somewhat that he would never love her, but it was a warm pain, a love pain. He couldn't be hurt by her if he didn't love her.

She felt him pull back from her and allowed her lids to lift halfway, her fingertips grazing the stubble on his chin.

"Your face is red where my beard scratched you." He frowned, his hand coming up to soothe the place.

She turned her face in to his hand to kiss the palm, feeling reckless and unfettered. "It doesn't hurt," she mumbled, just as her stomach started to growl.

Colin laughed, caressing her abdomen, then kissing the spot his hand had touched. "Now you're hungry for food. I'll have to feed you another way, then." He bit down on her chin. "How about ham and eggs and homemade raisin toast and pastry and—"

"Stop." Wyeth laughed, putting her finger to his lip, then watching while he nibbled on the tip. "I'll gain a hundred pounds if I eat all that."

"And I have fresh oranges for juice, and melon," Colin continued, still nibbling on her. "I'm going to take care of you. I'm going to make you strong again."

Wyeth looked at him, wide-eyed. There was no trace of amusement in the eyes that looked back at her, only determination. With one final hard kiss he rolled from her and off the bed. He stretched high into the air, his hands seeming to reach for the ceiling.

"I feel so damn good." He stared down at her, unselfconscious about his nakedness. "You make me feel this way, *petite.*"

She gazed at his body, feeling a hunger and a delight in his well-proportioned beauty, feeling proprietary about his width of shoulder, narrowness of hip, the arrow of chestnut hair that narrowed past his navel. She loved his long muscular legs, the sinewed thighs and calves, and his blatant masculinity that made her blood race.

"I like to look at you, too, love, but if I don't take a quick shower, we'll never eat, because I'll be back in bed with you. I can't get enough of you," he said in a slow, surprised way. Then he gave her a lopsided grin and ambled to the bathroom, whistling off-key.

Wyeth lay back against the pillow, relaxed, feeling as though she had been massaged. Not since the accident had she known such a feeling of well-being. She refused to think of the future or even as far ahead as the end of the snowstorm. She closed her eyes.

She woke to Colin's kissing of her eyelids and the smell of grilled tomatoes. He lifted her out of bed before she was fully awake, carried her to the bathroom door, patted her derriere, and closed the door on her. She was back out in minutes, her face washed, her body quickly rinsed with a Loofa and ravenous.

Colin helped her into a chair, kissing her lips. When the heat again built at once, he released her, his own breathing unsteady. "You have a power over me, *petite,* and that's the truth." He poured her juice from an iced jug, her coffee from a steaming silver pot.

Wyeth noticed that he seemed preoccupied. She hoped he was not having second thoughts about their lovemaking, because she had enjoyed it fully. His voice sounded loud in the quiet.

"*Petite,* there could be unforeseen effects from our night of love." He refilled her cup and buttered a croissant for her. "I feel a fool, but I have to tell you that I took no precautions last night. You filled my mind, nothing else."

Wyeth exhaled in relief. "I thought you were regretting last night." She felt her smile surface in response to his look of shock.

"You could never be more wrong, *petite,*" he growled at her, one hand reaching to wipe a crumb of croissant from her lips. "Still, there could be problems." He grinned at her.

"You don't have to worry." Wyeth looked at him, watching for his reaction. "When I was in the hospital, the doctors told Nate that there was a good chance I would never have children because of the extensive injuries."

"And this doesn't bother you?" Colin quizzed, in narrow-eyed concentration.

Wyeth shrugged. "I suppose it did at first, but I never expected that Nate and I would have children anyway, and so I came to accept it in a very easy way."

"Wouldn't you like to have children?" Colin asked, his voice soft.

Wyeth felt uncomfortable for a moment. "I have no desire for children now. If I wished for some, I would try to adopt. Adopting holds no problems for me."

"Me, either," Colin retorted, then began cleaning the table, not letting her help.

"Colin, please," she said, trying to edge her way to the sink while he playfully blocked her with his broad back.

He turned and took her hands in his soapy ones. "I want you to rest. You need it. When I'm through, I'm coming back to join you." Colin looked down at her, his eyes green velvet, not trying to hide his desire for her. Obediently she turned and headed for the bedroom.

Wyeth lay back dozing for a moment, then stretched and rose, heading for the bathroom.

She was half-asleep in the tub when Colin joined her, his hands and body reaching for her at once.

CHAPTER FIVE

For three days Wyeth refused to think beyond the moment, not wanting to accept that she was falling deeper in love with Colin every time she looked at him.

After the first day she felt no shyness in letting him see the places on her back and hip that were still slightly scarred. Far from being put off by the scars his mouth seemed to linger longest on them. He insisted on applying the soothing ointments that the Indians had given him. He was with her every minute. Wyeth felt as if some part of her self was missing when they were separated even for minutes. They slept together, ate together, cooked together.

On the third day they heard the roar of the plow that was coming from Montbel to rescue them.

"Rescue?" Colin muttered, his face twisted. "I was hoping for another blizzard." He held her in front of him, massaging her head with his chin. "I was hoping we would be here until spring," he laughed, but Wyeth could hear the grim note in his voice. She knew him well enough to know it was worry in his voice.

She had the same sense of foreboding. She had argued with herself all morning since the call had come that they would be sending a plow through.

Colin could have returned previously to Montbel on a snowmobile, but he wouldn't allow her to drive the other one, and he wouldn't leave her. His arms tightened across her breasts.

"Love." His lips pressed to her neck. "You're so beautiful, so fragile."

She turned in his arms, raising her hands to his face. "Not true. You've fattened me up. I can feel it." She smiled at him, then the smile faded as she saw such a naked look of desire in his eyes, a look of hunger so great that she reeled.

"Wyeth, do you have any regrets?" he whispered, his breath ruffling the curls on her head.

"None," she breathed, her one hand raising to his cheek. And it was true. She loved Colin with all her heart and would never regret a single moment of the time they had spent together. Whatever he felt for her, whatever he wanted of her, all of it didn't seem to matter much suddenly. But perhaps now was the time to bring things out in the open, before they returned to Montbel. It seemed to Wyeth that as long as they remained in this house nothing could ever go wrong between them.

"Colin, I—"

Before she could say more there was a banging on the door and a voice calling out in French. Colin answered in kind, and the mood was broken.

From then on time whirled. Colin left instructions on what was to be brought to Montbel, then supervised the dressing of Wyeth himself.

"Colin," she laughed, protesting. "I can't put on all those scarves. I won't be able to breathe."

"It's not that warm in the cab of the plow, and you're very subject to cold right now. Your resistance is down," he insisted, the mulelike look to his jaw telling her it was useless to argue.

He lifted her into the vehicle and then followed her, lifting her once more to settle her on his lap, making the driver, Jean, give her a sly look. Then he said something to Colin that Wyeth was sure was ribald by Colin's reluctant laugh and his admonition to the other man in French. The driver just shrugged, not too worried by the reprimand.

Wyeth put her mouth to Colin's ear. "What did he say?"

Colin looked her in the eye and shook his head, a smile pulling at his lips.

"Did he say I was your mistress?" Wyeth let her lips feather his ear again, crooning to him, feeling the restless move of his body.

"Nothing so blunt," he growled. "He told me he didn't blame me for dining on such a sweet piece, that the sweetest meat was nearest the bone." He grinned at her, the glitter in his eye making her pulse race. "Jean thinks you're too skinny, I'm sure."

Wyeth bit his ear, making him jump. His arms tightened on her body, one hand squeezing her thigh.

"If we were back at our house, I would pay you back for that." Colin whispered, the heat in his gaze telling her what form the payment would take.

In too short a time they were back at Montbel. It seemed to Wyeth that the whole family was there, all talking at once as usual. Colin shushed them all and said that Wyeth had to go to her room now, directing Émile Tiant to follow them.

Afterward all that Wyeth could remember was the malice that emanated from Amalie Colbert's eyes; then Marie was turning down her bed.

The last thing she remembered after Émile had given her a shot was Colin insisting that Wyeth be taken to McGill Medical Center for a complete physical workup and Émile trying to soothe him on her welfare.

She slept almost to the dinner hour, a clucking Marie laying out her clothes while she urged Wyeth to get to the bathroom where a hot tub was waiting.

"Madame, did you not see the flowers that Monsieur Colin has sent you." Marie pointed to the table near the window.

Wyeth lifted the spray of white roses to her face, noticing the envelope for the first time. She carried both flowers and note into the bathroom with her, not wanting Marie to see her kiss the flowers. She opened the note, a smile on her face, then crumpled the papers as disappointment coursed through her. Colin wasn't going to dine with her. He'd had to fly to Montreal on urgent business. He would return as soon as possible.

Wyeth stepped into the tub, sighing. As she lay there she pondered the sudden departure. She came to the conclusion that it had something to do with the stockholders' meeting tomorrow. She remembered Colin's tight-lipped visage when she had mentioned the meeting.

When she returned to the bedroom, Marie fussed her into a mauve silk dress that was a man-tailored shirt style on top with soft inverted pleats on the bottom. The only sophistication was the shimmering silk itself, which stirred at the slightest motion. With it she wore tiny circles of pink sapphire in her pierced ears and a matching pinkie ring that had belonged to Nate's grandmother. She wore black peau-de-soie sling pumps and carried a matching bag.

"Marie . . ." Wyeth hesitated. "Do I dine in the same place that I did the first evening?"

"Oh, *oui,* madame. There are not so many tonight, but Madame Solange and Dr. Émile will be there and of course Monsieur Kyle and Madame Mardi." She smiled at Wyeth, reaching out to pluck at the dress and straighten a fold.

Wyeth walked along the corridor leading to the family sitting room but saw no one. She continued on, coming into the mammoth lobby. She had not really explored its massiveness, but decided to take a few minutes and look it over now. She couldn't help staring upward at the fireplace, which was the focal point and dead center of the room. She shook her head at the crowds of people the six-sided monolith could accommodate on its spacious sides. When some of the people looked her way in friendly curiosity, she moved away, not wanting to be involved in a conversation where people might question her about her experience in the snow.

She frowned as she looked into one of the shop windows that lined the lobby. *Are you ashamed of your relationship with Colin?* she quizzed herself. *No!* she answered herself at once. *I'm not ashamed, but neither do I want to share any part of it with anyone else. It's ours!*

"How strange to see you making faces at yourself in that window!" Amalie purred next to her. "I cannot imagine myself doing such a thing. Perhaps you're more unwell than we thought." Amalie tapped Wyeth's arm with one purplish-red nail.

"Pull in your claws, Amalie," Wyeth said in frosted tones. "Excuse me, I'm going down to dinner."

"So am I." Amalie turned to accompany her, but her smooth voice didn't fool Wyeth. The woman disliked her as much as Wyeth disliked Amalie.

Wyeth didn't bother trying to converse with her. They descended the wide, graceful staircase in silence. For a moment Wyeth toyed with the idea of descending on the opposite side as Amalie when the stairs split, then decided that it would be childish.

To Wyeth's relief Kyle and Mardi were already at the table. Luc Colbert was also there, and the smile he gave Wyeth made her a little uncomfortable.

"Wyeth, darling, let me place you next to me," Luc said, his words making Mardi's eyebrows raise.

Wyeth felt a fluttering of anger but took the chair he proffered as Kyle rose and helped Amalie.

"How are you after your ordeal, Wyeth?" Mardi leaned across Luc to speak. "I was so frightened for you. It's very easy to lose yourself in the woods once it begins to snow."

Wyeth smiled at Mardi's real concern and told her that she felt better.

"How fortunate for Colin that he could keep Wyeth all to himself for a few days and convince her to vote with him at the meeting! Is it not, Kyle?" Amalie looked for a moment at Kyle, then down at the scrolled menu in her hand.

"Now, Amalie," Luc interjected softly. "I'm sure Wyeth can

think for herself." Luc squeezed Wyeth's hand, his eyes telling her that he thought Amalie a fool.

Wyeth tried to smile at him but fury at Amalie made her lips atrophy into a grimace, she was sure. She felt Mardi's worried look before she turned to the other woman and inquired about the children.

Mardi's deep breath of relief seemed to say that she was glad to be in familiar territory. "It's a full-time job, Wyeth. I'm glad I have Kyle's cousin to handle the gift shop for me. It wasn't so bad when there was just Annette. She was an angel, and it was fun to take her to the shop . . . but . . ." Mardi took a deep breath and rolled her eyes as she nodded to her waiter to put sour cream on her potato. "Little Nate is a different story. He's a hellion, Wyeth." She finished in a plaintive voice, making Wyeth laugh.

"I'm sure you can handle him. How old is he now?" Wyeth quizzed, aware of Luc's and Amalie's irritation at the trend of the conversation.

"He's three and a half going on twenty-one," Mardi sighed, looking morose when both Kyle and Wyeth laughed.

"Well, I have free time. I'd be glad to watch the children for you, or even take over in the gift shop," Wyeth assured Mardi.

"Wyeth, I love you. I'll take you up on it," Mardi said promptly.

"I think you'll be sorry, Wyeth," Amalie interjected. "I have never seen Nate without a grubby face, and hands to match." She shuddered.

Mardi's chin came up, ready to do battle for her cub, but Wyeth spoke first.

"I don't mind children, Mardi. I used to work in a day-care center to help pay my school expenses. Grubby hands don't scare me."

"Well, he is pretty bad," Mardi grudged, glaring at Amalie. "But I would be grateful to you."

"Don't tie up all Wyeth's time," Luc said in low tones. "I want the chance to show her around."

"Well, I've seen quite a bit of Montbel," Wyeth hurried to explain, seeing Kyle about to speak. Wyeth was sure that he was going to tell Wyeth that she needn't watch the children, and she wanted to forestall that. She needed something to fill up her time, to keep her from thinking of Colin and being forced to make a decision about their relationship.

After dinner Luc insisted that they all go down to the nightclub. He told Wyeth about the new band that had been installed and how danceable the big-band sound was.

Wyeth agreed to go when Kyle and Mardi said they would enjoy hearing the new group.

Dancing with Luc was a pleasant experience. He had a very controlled rather than rhythmic approach to the music. Wyeth had no trouble accommodating her steps to his.

"You're right, Luc. This music is good to dance to. I have to admit to a slight addiction to it fostered by my father," Wyeth laughed.

"You are very beautiful when you laugh," Luc whispered, his mouth close to her cheek.

He was not as tall as Colin, which made Wyeth wary in turning to look at him. His mouth was just a little above hers. When she tried to ease back from him, he only tightened his arms. "*Chérie,* you do something to me, do you know that?" Luc hissed into her hair.

"Don't be foolish," Wyeth blurted, pushing against his shoulder.

"Has my oh-so-popular cousin made inroads with you? Is that why you are so cold to me, *chérie*?" Luc scrutinized her face with narrowed eyes. "If so, I would advise you to develop a tough hide. My cousin Colin is well-known for his prowess with women."

"I'd really rather not hear you discuss Colin," Wyeth told him, tight-lipped.

His arms loosened all at once. "Ah, I see he has got to you. Enjoy it while you can, Wyeth. Amalie will let him have just so

106

much leeway; then she reels him in." He laughed, but there was no amusement in his eyes.

"You make him sound like a trout that she's having a tough time pulling in from the river," Wyeth said tartly, turning from him and going back to the table.

She was relieved when Kyle asked her to dance. She looked around the floor for Amalie. When she asked Kyle where she had gone, he just shrugged.

"Who knows where she goes, what she does, or what she thinks?" Kyle made a face. "If you've guessed that Amalie is not one of my favorite people, you've guessed right. She has given Mardi nothing but grief from the start, making remarks about her not being the right sort, as though the MacLendons and the Colberts were the chosen people." Kyle gave a rough laugh, but Wyeth could see the anger there. "Mardi and I met in college, and for me it was all over after the first look. I chased her until she gave in." Kyle leered down at Wyeth, making her laugh. "And things were fine here until Amalie decided to make a dead set at my brother after her husband died. Then she was here all the time." Kyle ground his teeth, looking somewhere over Wyeth's shoulder. The words seemed to erupt from his body. "God, what a viper that woman is. She makes comments about everything Mardi does. It's starting to have an effect on our marriage, I think," Kyle swallowed. "I wish that damned witch would disappear."

"Don't let her get to you, Kyle," Wyeth urged. "What you and Mardi have is rare. Mardi is more woman than Amalie will ever be," Wyeth finished, her voice harsh.

"Thanks. I think so, too, but sometimes my assurances aren't enough. If you don't mind, I'll quote you," Kyle whispered, leading her from the floor to the table.

They stayed for several dances, Amalie's absence seeming to give the party a lift. Mardi showed obvious signs of relief as she began to laugh more and urge Kyle to dance more.

Wyeth didn't even try to question how much lighter her own

107

spirit was without the other woman there. She didn't feel totally comfortable in Luc's company, but he was a good dancer, and he didn't mention Colin again. She was surprised to find that his taste in music was much like her own, and they vied to see how many "oldies" the band could play that the other wouldn't know. To Wyeth's chagrin he kept right up with her and requested some that she didn't know.

Mardi and Kyle entered the lists with a will, and though they didn't know many of the big-band oldies, they came out with a few.

Their laughter was infectious, and soon the table next to theirs began throwing titles to the band as well. It spread throughout the room until the bandleader said that he wouldn't be able to play them all. He decided that he would take one oldie from each table, but that it would have to be a true "oldie" or he wouldn't play it.

The laughter and the whistles and the hoots became louder than the music, as each table tried to stump the band.

When the band played "Good Night Sweetheart," many groaned, not wanting to give up the game.

"I didn't realize it was so late," Mardi moaned. "I'll never be able to handle those children of mine in the morning."

"I'll help you, love," Kyle soothed, saying good night to both Luc and Wyeth. "Wyeth, you're great fun."

"Thank you, Kyle; so are you, both of you." Wyeth grinned, accepting a hug from him and Mardi. "I'll come by around nine and relieve you of the two darlings for a while. Is that all right with you?"

"Oh, Wyeth, I hate to ask you when you're supposed to be resting . . . but . . ." Mardi sighed.

"You didn't ask. I offered. I mean it. I'll be at your rooms about nine." Wyeth pushed her toward her husband.

She turned to say good night to Luc, but he shook his head and led her toward the rathskeller instead of the stairs. "I'm tired, Luc, I really am. Tomorrow I'll be watching the children in the morning, and in the afternoon is the stockholders' meeting. . . ." Wyeth's voice trailed.

"A nightcap, that's all." He settled her into one of the oak chairs that were placed around the small tables near the fireplace, then went to the bar. He returned almost at once with two bottles of wine.

"Some nightcap!" Wyeth glared at him. "I'd rather have a Perrier and lime."

"You've had that all night. A nice light wine will help you sleep."

"I don't need help," Wyeth grudged, sipping at the clear liquid, her tongue reacting at once to the dryness by making her salivate. "I hope I don't sleep through the alarm."

"Why do you make trouble for yourself, Wyeth? Call Mardi, and tell her that you can't take care of her brats. That's her job."

"Don't be so pushy, Luc," Wyeth answered, disgruntled by his interference. "I want to watch them. Mardi works very hard. She can use a break."

Luc twisted the stem of his glass between thumb and forefinger, looking down at the swirling liquid. "How do you intend to vote tomorrow?"

"I'm not sure. It's rather an odd time of year to have a stockholders' meeting, isn't it?" Wyeth hedged.

Luc smiled at her avoidance of the issue. "Yes. A board meeting was held to decide if the owners should allow the building of condominiums on the property for the purpose of turning more of the holdings into resort land. The voting was split, and Colin pushed through a motion that a special meeting should be held to let the stockholders vote on the issue," Luc finished in a flat tone. "Colin wants to stop the progress of Montbel, which would bring in vast revenues to the stockholders. If you vote with him, you'll deny them increased monies."

"You'll be voting with the group that wants the condos?" Wyeth asked, taking another sip of wine.

"Yes. So will Amalie. Vote with us, Wyeth. It's to your advantage as well."

Wyeth rose to her feet, placing her hand on his shoulder to keep him from rising. "I'm going to bed, Luc. I'm tired. I'll make my decision tomorrow. Good night."

She was out of the room before he could make a move. Wyeth didn't bother with the elevator but took the wide stairs that would take her close to her first-floor room.

Beau was there to greet her, but she hardly noticed him even when she attached his leash and walked him in the enclosed area outside her window. As usual, he leaped and bucked against the leash. She sighed but kept talking to him, trying to keep him calm. Colin had told her that she would never make him like the leash. She was beginning to believe him. She was bending down in front of the dog, petting him, talking to him, when she heard the phone ringing in her room. The sound barely penetrated to the outside, so she wasn't sure it was the first ring. She sprinted for her room, spending time pulling off her gloves to get the door open. By the time she reached her room, the caller had given up.

"Well, Beau, I hope you're satisfied." She spoke crossly to the tail-wagging wolf cub. "If you had been a good boy and not entangled me in your leash, I might have made it to the phone."

Beau jumped into her lap, snow and all, making Wyeth squeal.

"Monster!" She pushed at him to free herself, then rose from the brocade bedroom chair that was now splotched with wet snow. "Look what you've done!" Wyeth pointed to the chair. "That's right, sit there and laugh. Marie will rip at me tomorrow, not you. Oh, don't try to make up, oaf." Wyeth tried not to laugh, but he looked so comical with his ears falling forward and his big feet splaying everywhere. "You're a living, breathing disaster area, and I don't know why I keep you." She looked at the telephone for long moments. "Do you think it was Colin, Beau? I miss him so much, yet I'm afraid to face him when he returns." She sighed and dried the dog, letting him follow her to

110

the bathroom where she took a quick sponge. She turned around when she heard gagging sounds behind her and found the dog frothing at the mouth. She gasped before she realized that Beau had taken her bar of Pears soap from the side of the sunken tub and tried to eat it.

"You great fool, give me that. Oh, Lord, look at you. It serves you right." She laughed as the dog spewed bubbles from his mouth, a surprised look on his face. "Here, let me wash your mouth. What will you do next?"

After she settled the dog, Wyeth climbed into the big bed, trying to imagine that Colin was beside her. She hugged the other pillow to her and closed her eyes.

She surfaced in stages from sleep, the telephone ringing close to her ear. "Yes," she mumbled, her mouth woolly.

"Where were you when I called before?" Colin's question was brusque in her ear.

Fuzzily she tried to stare at the clock radio. "Colin, it's four o'clock in the morning!" She yawned, almost cracking her jaw.

"I know what time it is. I'm flying to Montbel in an hour. Answer my question. Where were you when I called before? You should have been in bed. Where were you?" he barked.

"Walking Beau." She yawned and answered without thinking. Then she sat bolt upright. "Where do you get off talking to me in that tone?" she snapped back, trying to swallow another yawn but failing.

His throaty laugh made her sink back against the pillows. "Are you in bed, darling?" he crooned, no trace of his earlier harshness in his voice.

"Y—yes," she sighed, knowing that when he took that tone with her, she could not stay angry for very long.

"God, I wish I were there with you. Go back to sleep." He rang off before Wyeth could speak. Weak with longing for him, she replaced the receiver and slid down under the silk comforter, sure she would never go back to sleep.

She peeled back the layers of sleep again when she heard a

voice whispering in her ear and a smooth, hard body curving around hers. When she felt questing fingers feathering her thighs, her eyes snapped open and she looked into Colin's amused face. "Oh, darn, for a minute there, I thought you were Paul Newman, and I got all excited," Wyeth muttered, one finger scratching at his beard.

"Oh, you did, did you? Damn you, Wyeth; I'll teach you to expect just one man in your bed—me," he growled, the gleam of amusement hardening just a bit as he pressed her back into the pillows, his body fitting to hers like the missing piece of a puzzle.

Wyeth gasped, trying to keep on keel so that she could chastise him for being such a bear when he called. She tried. She failed. Instead she gathered him to her hungry body, not trying to mask her need of him.

Her nerve endings were laid bare for him. Each touch was like a flame to kindling, until she could no longer control her responses to him. A detached part of Wyeth was appalled at the scope of her surrender to him. Nothing was held back, and the sounds of their groans mingled in the quiet room. Their bodies couldn't get close enough. Yet Colin didn't hurry. He seemed to take delight in her toes, her calves, behind her knees . . . "Darling, I love that perfume you use." He groaned, his tongue touching her thigh. "Does it satisfy you to know that you're driving me out of my mind?"

"Yes." Wyeth tried to respond in a steady voice and failed. She tried to say more, but the only thing that came from her throat was a sigh. Then she knew no more, as light seemed to explode behind her eyes. She wondered for a dazed moment how Colin could continue to make their lovemaking more and more exciting. There was a hazy sureness that she couldn't climb to any more plateaus. Then she seem to melt into him, and the light was all around them.

Her body slid along his as she relaxed against him, her eyes still closed, feeling his one hand push the damp curls back from her forehead.

"Damn you, Wyeth. I can't stay away from you." Colin sighed. "Mrs. Arbuthnot, whom Tante Cecile lives with, said that I was like a caged lion when I was with her in Montreal. She said she was glad to give me proxy just to get rid of me." He smiled down at her. "She also told me that she knew I had woman trouble. Take care of it, she said. So here I am, in bed with my trouble."

Wyeth hit him with her pillow. In seconds they had a battle in progress, an excited Beau barking through the glass doors from the outside. "We had better stop," she gasped, laughing down at Colin as she lay across him. "He won't stop barking until we settle down. I won." She smirked at him, holding his head between her hands and pressing him to the bed.

"No way," Colin asserted, flipping her onto her back. "I win."

"Not fair. You cheated." Wyeth struggled with him, feeling a wonderful sense of rightness. She let her hands feather up his cheek, tug at his beard, then downward to his chest.

"Who's cheating now? Let's face it, lady. In any battle between us you have all the weapons," he growled as he lowered himself onto her, his breath coming in short breaths as she continued to caress him.

"True. But you are a very worthy opponent, my own," Wyeth murmured, surrendering to the gathering storm.

Their lovemaking was shattering to both of them, and Wyeth knew that Colin's bemused look was echoed in her own face. "It makes you weak, but still you feel as though you could get to the moon without a rocket," she whispered as he held her close.

"Lady, you never said a truer word. Now, get your lovely tush out of this bed. We have to shower. It wouldn't look good for the man who called this special meeting to be late." They showered together, washing each other with great care.

Wyeth laughed as Colin left the shower muttering that if he didn't leave now, he never would. Wyeth felt like Wonder Woman. "Colin?" She called to him as she was sitting in front of the vanity applying makeup and he was trimming his beard. "Do you think it would be too out of character if I dragged you into the meeting by the hair and then gave a Tarzan yell?"

Colin appeared in her mirror. "I can't allow it. You'll ruin my image."

She shook her head, smiling, but she could feel her skin tingling as Colin assessed her body in the mirror, his eyes approving the apricot-colored bra and panties in the sheerest silk.

"The first chance we get, we're going to fly to Montreal and get you more of those undies. You look delicious." His tone was idle, but his eyes weren't.

Wyeth hurried him, knowing it wouldn't take much to get her back to bed. She knew when she had the time to think about it, she would be appalled at her reactions to Colin.

The meeting went smoothly at first. Wyeth felt a swelling pride as she watched Colin handle the meeting with aplomb and a business knowledge that she was sure would have impressed Mr. Wingate, had he been there. About halfway through Luc and his contingent made a move for control, bringing forth an impressive number of voters who wanted the condominium project to pass. The arguments on both sides were detailed and well thought out, but she thought that Colin's argument for the environment and the preservation of the seigneury were the most meaningful, and she was glad that she had thrown her votes with him.

It was only after the vote was taken that Wyeth realized Colin hadn't said a word or even given a glance in her direction, which she could interpret as an attempt to influence her. Considering how much the outcome of the vote mattered to him, and of course, how easily he could have exerted his considerable influence, Wyeth was a bit surprised. Oh, he knew she was stubborn —the type who might even take a stand in opposition to him just to prove her autonomy. Had he judged it best to let her make up her mind on her own? Or was he simply sure of her feelings for him, so much an egotist that he had not even considered the possibility of her siding with the opposition.

He should be pleased at any rate, Wyeth thought. It didn't take a political genius to see that her votes could have turned the outcome either way. She felt relieved. Now that this issue had been settled, perhaps she would be better able to sort out her relationship with Colin.

In the end Colin won, but not by a large margin. Wyeth had the chance to see the cold anger on both Amalie's and Luc's faces, seated as she was in the back.

"What do you think of your Colin now, Wyeth?" Tante Cecile was leaning on the arm of Bill Balmain, another woman with her.

"He isn't my Colin." Wyeth blushed, angry at the quick reaction of her body to the question. "I thought he did well, Tante."

"Oh, yes, he always does well." She shrugged one small lace-clad shoulder. "I think today he was perhaps even a little *dramatique*. You think, Bill, he was trying to impress someone?" The old lady looked at Wyeth and nodded.

Bill smiled at Wyeth and introduced her to Tante Cecile's companion, Mrs. Arbuthnot. As Wyeth was acknowledging the introduction she felt an arm at her waist. Thinking it was Colin, she leaned into the arm. It tightened at once, pulling her close before she could even turn her head.

"Wyeth, my sweet, I should be angry with you for giving your votes to Colin, but how could I ever be angry with you." Luc's voice jerked Wyeth's body, but he didn't allow her to pull away from him. "Tante, Madame Arbuthnot, Bill, what a family gathering we have. Are you all coming in for the luncheon?"

"Luc." Colin's voice cut through the group. "Your little group has been buying stock." His voice was low, but Wyeth was sure she wasn't the only one that knew Colin was in a rage. "Cousin, if you want war, I'll give it to you. In fact, after today I'd welcome it." Colin looked from Luc's face to the arm that was still around Wyeth.

She held her breath. Colin swept her with a murderous look, his gaze settling on Luc. She managed to pull free from Luc, her eyes still on Colin, but he didn't look away from Luc. The silence seemed to stretch and strain over the minutes, making it like hours.

"Colin, darling, I should be angry with you." Amalie pouted, then sighed. "But then, you always did go your own way whether you were right or wrong. Come along; shouldn't we be going along to the dining room now?" Amalie smiled up at him, taking his arm. "Bill, do take Wyeth. I know Luc wants to speak to Tante and Madame Arbuthnot." Amalie's red lips stretched across her face, making Wyeth want to tear at them.

"Managing again are you, Amalie?" Colin's lips curled, his anger not abated.

Wyeth's temper began to heat as Colin continued to ignore her. Adding fuel to the fire, he allowed Amalie to lead him away toward the dining room. Wyeth had all she could do not to raise the vase of roses from the rosewood side table and fling it at his retreating back. She hardly heard Bill Balmain's comments as he led her behind Tante, Madame Arbuthnot, and Luc.

CHAPTER SIX

The days and weeks following the stockholders' meeting were fraught with tension for Wyeth. She had torn into Colin when they had returned to her suite the evening of the meeting, neither of them seeming to care how the other was struck and wounded. She had forgotten everything but the raw, burning hurt inside herself, because Colin had turned from her and stayed with Amalie for the rest of the day.

"Who are you to tell me how to behave?" he'd roared back. "What kind of show was that you were putting on, first with Luc, then with Bill? You were acting like a damn tease."

"And you would damn well know about that," Wyeth yelped, "with that bitch you had on your arm the whole day."

"Wyeth, behave yourself," he bellowed, making Beau whine. "Talk like a lady, and act like one."

"Don't you tell me how to act, you—you pompous idiot! How dare you yell at me!" She raised both fists in the air, flailing them in his direction. "If I were a man, I'd pound you three feet into the ground."

"Well, if you were a man, you'd be on your back by now, you nasty-tongued little rogue." Colin's chin came out, his eyes sparkling. "And if I ever catch you—"

"Don't you threaten me," Wyeth interrupted in sepulchral tones, her voice lowered a full decibel. "Out of this room. Out now." She pointed, her body feeling red hot with anger.

"Damn right I will. I wouldn't stay here if you begged me,"

he thundered, scooping his jacket from the bed. The door shook in its frame, he slammed it so hard.

That night Wyeth alternately soaked her pillow and punched it, threatening never to speak to him again as long as she lived, vowing to sell her shares to Luc, promising . . . She fell asleep with her brain in a whirl, only to waken hours later and remain awake for the rest of the night. She slept toward dawn.

The next day she woke, head woolly, her eyes puffy and with yellowish and blue bags beneath them. She prayed she wouldn't run into Dr. Tiant until she looked better.

Before Marie brought her breakfast she called Mardi and offered to watch the children. An ecstatic Mardi assured her that nine thirty was not too early to stop by for the children.

So for two weeks Wyeth cared for the children. Much to her surprise, she found it fun and looked forward to the days with them. For over a week now she had been arranging to have breakfast with them in the big dining room, and though Mardi had tried to dissuade Wyeth from doing it, hinting at the un-named horrors Nate might perform, Wyeth had had good luck with the children. She knew they liked her as well, and now as Annette came roaring down the hall toward her, her little arms outstretched, Wyeth felt a sting of tears behind her eyes. She hugged the five-year-old to her and tried to listen to the outpourings of things that had happened in the twelve hours they had been apart.

". . . and Nate poured his porridge on Cat, Tante Wyeth," Annette announced, taking a deep breath.

"Oh, there you are, Wyeth." Mardi leaned against the doorjamb, rolling her eyes. "He's in rare form today. Are you sure you want to take him? Last night he wanted to show Colin his new Fisher-Price truck and threw it across the room. If Colin hadn't had such good reflexes, he would have had a whopping big lump on his skull today."

Wyeth smiled to cover the wrench she felt at the mention of Colin's name. She lifted her chin, cursing the feeling that made her so weak at the sound of his name. Weak wasn't the word, she thought.

"Wyeth, are you sure you feel up to this? You look a little pale this morning." Mardi straightened from the door to the apartment and watched Wyeth as she entered the room, Annette clutching one hand. "How long have you been here at Montbel, Wyeth?"

"Six weeks yesterday." Wyeth smiled at the younger woman. "Why?" Wyeth turned to laugh at Nate who was roaring at her from his playpen, shouting, "*Y, Y, Y, Y* " in comic repetition. Wyeth knew he was calling her and crooned to him that she was coming.

". . . because I don't know what I did before you came. You are marvelous with the children, and they love you. Kyle has said how their behavior has improved because you take such an interest in what they do. Annette can't stop talking at night about her days, and the same holds true for Mighty Mouse over there." Mardi looked toward the playpen, then gave a squeal and jumped forward to rescue the cross-eyed Siamese cat who was being pulled through the bars by a determined Nate. The yowling, shouting, squeaking had Wyeth collapsing in a chair laughing. Mardi glared at her as she set the ruffled cat down a safe distance from the glowering Nate. "How can you laugh at him, Wyeth?" Mardi quizzed in disgust as she handed Wyeth his jacket. Wyeth buckled the little harness on Nate that allowed her to keep him in check, and then led the children from the room, waving an airy good-bye to their mother.

"Wyeth," Mardi called. "You didn't tell me how you were feeling. Colin asked me the same thing. Don't you see him anymore?"

"Too busy," Wyeth answered ambiguously, rushing the children into the elevator. She looked at the picture of Montbel on the wall of the lift, answering Nate's gibberish and Annette's endless questions in monosyllables. *No, I don't see him anymore,* she thought. *He avoids me. He'd rather be with Amalie, no doubt.*

119

I never see him except—well, maybe just glimpses in the halls or lobby—once at the curling barn, once at the rathskeller, several times while dining. Each time it seemed Amalie was at his side or nearby. They had nodded to each other, not speaking. Wyeth had avoided looking at Amalie's triumphant face.

"You don't want to talk to me, do you, Aunt Wyeth?" Annette lisped, a forlorn face upturned to Wyeth.

Wyeth bent over the child, contrite. "I'm sorry, darling, I–I was thinking about our breakfast."

"Porrish," Nate thundered, scowling at Annette when she tried to shush him. "Porrish," he repeated in a lower register, his lip jutting forth.

Wyeth swept him up into her arms, laughing at him. "Of course you shall have your porridge, darling; with sliced peaches, if you like."

"Ugh!" Annette scoffed as the elevator doors parted. "That's barf. Danielle says that porridge is barf." Her lisp was like a clarion call, making Nate yowl in anger as he flailed his pudgy arms to reach his offending sister.

Wyeth stumbled from the lift with the wriggling child, right into Colin's arms.

"Easy, Wyeth." Colin spoke to her but smiled at the beaming Nate, who held his arms out to his uncle. "I'll carry him for you. Hello, Annette. Yes, *petite,* I'll take your hand."

"And will you eat with us, Uncle Colin? I want to ask Aunt Wyeth to take us to the pool today, but she doesn't like to swim, I don't think," Annette caroled, skipping next to her uncle. "Nate is bad, Uncle Colin. He spills his food," she announced, satisfied when her brother's lip quivered with rage.

"Porrish," Nate bellowed again just as they were descending to the dining room, making many of the guests laugh, especially those who had seen the chubby little boy at other breakfasts. When he heard the adults titter, Nate looked around wide-eyed, his two fingers in his mouth. His hand dropped as he gummed and grinned widely at the diners.

Wyeth was glad for Marcel's directions to the other waiters. He always seemed to know just what would distract the children. Today there was a plate of orange slices in the shape of faces, with grapes for eyes and slivers of prune for eyebrows. The children took delight in cannibalizing their smiling faces on the plate, and Wyeth had no trouble getting Nate to have his fruit before his beloved "porrish."

She was glad that she had to concentrate on Nate when he was eating. She was far too conscious of Colin at her side, feeling his eyes roving over her. She saw Colin gesture to Marcel from the corner of her eye.

"But Monsieur Colin, I have wanted Pierre and Jean to feed the *enfants*, but Madame insists on doing it herself." Marcel's shrug managed to convey that he was hurt by this and that he also considered Madame out of her mind.

"Madame will let Jean and Pierre feed them today," Colin pronounced, gesturing to the two hovering waiters. Then he turned to Wyeth. "I think we need some time to talk. Oh, I know this isn't the place or the time, but I never see you anymore. Even when I send for you, you don't come."

"Why should I be at your beck and call?" Wyeth inquired, her tones aloof, as she dipped her spoon into the grapefruit. Her hand paused halfway between iced bowl and mouth. "When did you send for me?"

Colin's look was irritated as he sipped the black-as-a-well French coffee. "Don't play games, Wyeth. Last Friday night there was a cocktail party for some friends that I wanted you to meet. My secretary said that Amalie contacted you herself and invited you and you flatly refused, that you said you didn't wish to meet my friends."

"And you believed that? You couldn't check with me person-ally to see if I would come?" Wyeth asked, her breathing deepen-ing as temper surfaced.

"I was in Montreal all last week, as you know—"

"I didn't know. How could I? You don't discuss your days with me. You rarely speak to me," she shot back.

"And is that my fault?" He leaned across the table and hissed, as though aware of Annette's glances. "When I approach you, you usually turn your back and walk away."

"That's untrue," Wyeth said, jabbing butter into a flaky croissant and mangling it. Marcel's tut-tutting at her shoulder only added fuel to the fire. "I refuse to discuss your reprehensible behavior in front of the—"

"My what?" Colin's muted roar made Nate look up from his "porrish," his one hand swinging the spoon of oatmeal in a wide arc to drop the contents on his outraged sister.

The ensuing uproar, which had all the niceties of a blood feud, demanded Wyeth's full attention as she tried to placate the children and the incensed waiters who blamed each other's charges for the mishap.

"Damn this mess," Colin muttered, surging to his feet. In a few succinct French phrases he had reduced the waiters to silence and the children to hiccuping obedience. With one last baleful look at Wyeth he strode off, not answering the greetings sent his way from the other diners.

Wyeth couldn't tear her eyes from that retreating back. Beautiful shouldn't describe a man, but to Wyeth that was how Colin was to her. It was more than looks, the surface of the man, it was the fabric of him, the essence that she loved, every spiritual nuance that made him Colin MacLendon. How had everything gone bad between them? More bad luck, she thought.

It was Nate's yowling demand that she get him out of the high chair that pulled Wyeth's attention back to the children.

With a sigh of relief Wyeth left the dining room, aware of the smiles of the other diners and the pained looks of Pierre, Jean, and especially, Marcel.

She was so rattled that she agreed to take the children to the pool. She was in the locker room changing them into the swimsuits that the attendant had provided for them.

122

"No, Annette, I don't need a suit to watch you swim, and you don't want to wait until I run to my suite and fetch mine, now do you?"

The pouting Annette's black curls bobbed as she shook her head. "But I want you to swim, Aunt Wyeth."

"Shwim," Nate roared into Wyeth's ear, his chubby arms encircling her neck, his sticky lips landing on her cheek.

"Darling, I'll swim another day," Wyeth hedged, trying to control the fear that began slowly to mount.

"Ahem," the attendant interrupted, handing Annette her own fluffy towel. "I have a choice of suits, madame. The suit will, of course, become your own to take home, after your stay at Montbel is over."

"Aunt Wyeth is not going to leave Montbel." Annette pouted, retreating to clutch Wyeth by the leg.

"Not leave," Nate bellowed, managing a stranglehold on Wyeth's neck that prevented her from telling the attendant not to bother bringing out the suits.

Before Wyeth could say anything the attendant, whose name was Matilde, was spreading an assortment of suits on the room-long mirrored dressing table. Wyeth saw the names Speedo and Head on the boxes. It was easier to choose than to argue. She only hoped the suit would cover her scars.

She left the children in the care of the attendant while she changed into the V-necked tank suit in pale blue that was similar to the racing suits she had worn when she had competed. She had noticed the Jordache and Arena labels as well but decided on the simplest style she could find.

She had no idea how provocative she looked until Matilde looked at her in open admiration.

"Ah, madame, the lifeguards will be watching you and not the swimmers."

"Shwim," Nate chirped, not letting her change her mind as he tugged her toward the door.

In the pool area Wyeth felt the rush of bile to her throat as the ever present fear took hold of her. She took deep breaths leading the children to the shallow end, which still worried her. The shallow end would still be too deep for the children to stand.

Annette tugged her hand harder and led her to another area that housed a shallow wading pool.

Wyeth gave a sigh of relief. She wouldn't even need to be near the Olympic-size pool which figured so prominently in her dreams of diving into fire, or even look at it. Determined to ignore its existence, she took a chair so that her back would be toward the bigger water area and yet she could watch the children in the wading pool.

She was beginning to relax when Annette approached her and said that she wanted to go to the bathroom. Wyeth was about to get Nate out of the pool so that she could take them both when a woman guest assured Wyeth that she could watch both Nate and her little boy with no trouble. Wyeth was loath to leave him and tried to explain to the other woman how active Nate was.

"Don't be silly. I can watch him," the other woman insisted, a little testy now.

"Aunt Wyeth, I have to go," Annette wailed.

"All right, dear. Are you sure . . ." Wyeth's voice trailed as the other woman's eyebrows rose and Annette pulled at her hand.

With one last, anxious look at Nate, who seemed to be absorbed in play with his new friend Billy, Wyeth shepherded Annette to the lady's locker room, where the rest rooms were located.

With Wyeth rushing her Annette didn't have as much time as she would have liked to play in the sink while washing her hands.

Wyeth had a sense of doom as she heard the hysterical chatter coming from the pool area as she hurried Annette down the corridor leading to the pool.

"How did I know he would climb up there? That child is a monster. My Billy would never do such a thing. I would never have agreed to watch him if his mother had told me what an

124

incorrigible child he was . . ." The woman continued, seeming not to need oxygen, as she talked without a break.

Wyeth looked at the woman in growing horror as both she and the lifeguard and several others looked upward toward the three-meter board.

Wyeth closed her eyes for a moment in silent prayer, but she didn't need Annette's clarion voice to tell her that Nate had somehow made it to the top of the ladder and was now toddling out to the end of the board.

"He'll fall, Aunt Wyeth." Annette's high-pitched shriek made Nate totter.

Wyeth could see his lower lip jut out as the woman tried to clutch her arm and explain that she thought Nate was a subnormal specimen—nothing like her dear Billy.

Wyeth shook off her arm, wanting to fling her into the pool for not watching Nate. Yet she blamed herself for not taking the child with her in the first place.

The lifeguard was whispering in her other ear that he had set off the alarm, that the front desk would have already contacted the fire department.

"And you think Nate is going to peaceably wait for the firemen to arrive, do you?" Wyeth snapped at him, then turned back to look up at Nate and assure him that Auntie Wyeth was coming to get him. She turned back to the guard, biting off each word. "Watch him. If he starts to fall get in the water and get under him. Don't let him sink, or I'll drown you myself."

Wyeth went to the ladder and started a slow climb, speaking to Nate in low tones. She was almost to the top when she heard the familiar voice.

"What the hell . . . ?" Then there was a heavy silence, then whispered instructions.

Wyeth kept climbing, reminding herself of how many times she had climbed to the top of a three-meter just for the fun of sailing into the air and hitting the water clean.

She could feel the first beadings of moisture on her upper lip.

125

The wet trickle from her underarm was cold. Her hands had a slippery feel on the metal railing as she forced her body upward. She could hear the murmur of the crowd now. She was lifted off the ladder by her thoughts, carried down to the starting blocks affixed at the end of the pool. She bit her lips until she tasted blood. She would not be diving into flames! This was reality, not the nerve-rending nightmare that had been her constant companion for so long. She had no time to dwell on her own fears. She was climbing to get Nate, to bring him down, unharmed and unafraid. She was going to do just that.

At the top she paused, taking a deep breath, watching Nate who was sideways to her, looking down to the deck of the pool where all the people were looking up at him. It had never seemed quite as high to Wyeth.

In her peripheral vision she saw the motion that was Colin flinging off his jacket, shouting hard words at the guard and the people who lined the deck.

"Auntie Wyeth's here, darling." She spoke in measured tones to Nate. "Stay there, and don't move. I'm coming to take you down."

With a steady, calm step she surely didn't feel, Wyeth moved out onto the board. She swallowed in a throat dry as the desert as she imagined the physical and/or psychological hurt that Nate could suffer if he fell from such a height.

Wyeth was an arm's reach away when Billy's mother screamed at Wyeth to grab Nate.

Nate started, looked at Wyeth, tottered for a moment, and fell.

Wyeth leaped, catching him around the waist, but she couldn't keep her balance. She felt her bad hip strike the board as she tumbled, then they were falling. Wyeth only had milliseconds to cuddle the boy to her body and take the blow on the water for both of them, then she struck the water, back and shoulders first, knocking the air clean from her body before the water closed over her head.

Years of stringent training took over as she kicked at once to the surface, dazedly aware that she had to get Nate into the air. Then she felt him pulled from her hands and lifted even as her arm was being pulled upward. One hand flung the hair from her eyes as she surfaced, watching the guard lift Nate into Émile Tiant's arms. When Nate started to yowl, Wyeth started to cry.

"Don't cry, darling. He's all right," Colin whispered in her ear as he lifted her to the side of the pool, hoisted himself to the deck, then lifted Wyeth beside him.

"Auntie Wyeth, why are you crying?" Annette wailed. "Is Nate going to die? Billy's momma says he could die falling from there."

"Everyone is fine now, *petite*," Colin said, his voice of authority giving instant reassurance. Somehow he had a towel and was wrapping Wyeth in it, but she didn't look. She just stared down at Émile Tiant as he spoke gently to the wide-eyed Nate, who stared at the circle of people with his two fingers in his mouth. He saw Wyeth and removed the fingers.

"Lunth," he thundered, his lisp more pronounced than usual.

"Oh, darling," Wyeth sobbed. "I'm going to get you the biggest lunch."

Nate nodded, wriggling free of the laughing Émile, to lift his arms to Wyeth.

There was a flurry at the door, and Mardi and Kyle came forward looking grim and white-faced as they reached for their son.

Colin explained all in succinct terms, and Wyeth felt more tears when Mardi and Kyle both hugged her and told her not to blame herself.

Wyeth hadn't had much time to consider the question of blame. But now that the flurry of excitement was over, upsetting thoughts began to surface. It was no one's fault really; if anyone was to blame clearly, it was Billy's mother, who should have kept a closer eye on Nate. But still, whenever Wyeth considered how tragic the outcome of this little misadventure might have been, she could not dismiss the thought that somehow she had caused it all. Her uncanny ability to bring misfortune to those around her had seemed to have surfaced once more. Why did it seem that she was always at the center of these things? The rational, logical mind she had always been proud of was beginning to accept this most irrational thought. Could it be true? Was it really her awful fate to be a jinx to those she loved? No—it was impossible. She wouldn't allow herself to think that way. Why, if ever she thought such a horrible notion to be true, she didn't know what she would do; she didn't know if she could go on living.

She felt Colin's warm hand on her shoulder again and turned to look up at him. His tender expression filled her with an incredible sadness. "Wyeth, my dear, are you sure you're all right? You look very pale, as if—"

"Stop clucking over me like a mother hen, Colin," she said forcing a smile. "I'm fine, really."

Among the few remaining bystanders Wyeth heard the voice of Billy's mother rising over the din, and both she and Colin turned to listen. "No, indeed. I shouldn't think you could blame anyone for that incorrigible child." Billy's momma began giving Billy a complacent pat on the head. "There are some children that are just impossible to handle . . ." Her voice trailed as a wild-eyed Wyeth rounded on her and started toward her, her fists clenched.

The woman gave a muted squeak as Colin caught hold of Wyeth and dragged her back. She disappeared out of the pool area as a muttering Wyeth cursed her and her progeny roundly. She was still straining in Colin's hold, her eyes on the pool door, when Colin whispered in her ear, amusement in his voice.

"The last time I heard language like that I was in a locker room with some men."

"Drat that stupid woman," Wyeth hissed, allowing herself to be led toward the locker room. She felt Colin's mouth at her neck and forgot Billy's momma.

She was in the locker room with Mardi while they waited for

dry clothes, Annette announcing to anyone who entered what her brother had done. Nate's fingers were back in his mouth, and his eyes were fluttering in a relaxed semidoze.

As an elderly lady walked in Annette turned to the fresh audience at once. "My Auntie Wyeth was going to sock Billy's momma," she pronounced with bloodthirsty satisfaction. "My brother, Nate, flewed off the diving board. Auntie Wyeth flewed, too."

The elderly guest looked with disfavor on a half-dressed Wyeth, still rubbing her hair dry. Wyeth tried to smile at the woman, but the other's palpable disapproval made communication a waste of time.

Mardi had one hand over her mouth, trying not to laugh. "You are going to be the talk of Montbel. Most of the ones in Tante Cecile's age range will consider you a rowdy," Mardi hissed, not able to mask a burble of laughter when Wyeth glared at her. "All because of my darlings you will become the 'Wild Woman of Montbel.' "

"It wasn't their fault if that stupid woman was careless." Wyeth hugged Annette and rubbed her finger down Nate's cheek. His eyes were closed in sleep.

"You had better marry Colin and save your good name," Mardi babbled happily, not noticing the look of strain on Wyeth's face.

"I'm not going to marry Colin." Wyeth cleared her throat trying to keep her voice steady.

"Oh, but you should," Mardi stated, round-eyed. "I've never seen him look at any woman the way he looks at you. Kyle agrees with me."

Wyeth hurried into her clothes. "Don't get that idea into your head, Mardi. Neither Colin nor I wish to marry each other," Wyeth said. *At least, he wouldn't want to marry me,* she thought, then pulled herself up short, shaking her head. *No, don't even think of marrying him. Even if he wanted to, I wouldn't.*

"What is it, Wyeth? You look so white. Aren't you feeling

well?" Mardi quizzed, rising with the sleeping Nate in her arms, refusing to let Wyeth take him from her. "You're still recuperating from your stay in the hospital." She frowned at Wyeth. "Maybe you've been doing too much with my kids, wearing yourself down. Oh God, Colin will kill me if you get sick again. I'd hate myself if you became ill because of me."

"Don't be silly," Wyeth reprimanded, finishing with her makeup and allowing Annette to put a little lip gloss on her mouth, then taking the child by the hand and following Mardi from the room.

Émile was still there talking with Kyle and Colin. "Mardi, I would like you to bring him to see me tomorrow. I don't think there will be any adverse effects, but I'd like to check him anyway." Émile shrugged, then turned to look at Wyeth. "You, I would like to see as well. Arrange it with my nurse."

Wyeth was about to protest when Colin intervened. "I'll arrange it with Clotilde myself, Émile, and I will see that she is on time for her appointment."

Wyeth rounded on him to argue, then gasped at the look on his face. He was masking nothing, letting his feelings for her show through in the sensual looks he was giving her. Wyeth could feel heat rise in her face as she caught the smug look Mardi was giving Kyle. "I have to help Mardi feed the children their lunch, then give them their nap," Wyeth explained, her voice hoarse.

"Fine, I'll help you," Colin pronounced in a bland tone, scooping Annette into his arms and making her laugh.

A sleepy Nate opened his eyes, glared at his mother, and roared, "Lunth."

Mardi poked Kyle when he laughed at his frowning son, but she couldn't hold back a smile of parental pride when the little boy reached two chubby arms out to his father so that he, too, could be carried piggyback down the hall.

Émile fell in step with Mardi and Wyeth, informing them that

130

he and Solange would be dining at Montbel that evening and that Solange had told him to contact Mardi.

Mardi nodded when Wyeth looked at her in a puzzled way. "Solange considers it one step higher than hell to have to sit with Amalie when they dine here."

Wyeth bit her lip, but Émile caught the smile. He shook his head, giving that Gallic shrug that was so much a part of him. "My Solange is not her most discreet in the company of the beautiful Amalie. I have told her that she must be more restrained, but—"

"Amalie is the one who provokes Solange," Mardi defended.

"But my Solange could ignore her, but this she does not do." Émile spoke in an indulgent tone, but there was a worry crease between his eyes.

He excused himself to catch up to the men when Annette told him that he was to sit with her.

"What Émile doesn't understand is that Amalie isn't a woman. She's a viper. Like most men, except my Kyle, he doesn't see that." Mardi lowered her voice. "The dear Amalie made a dead set at Émile once while she was still married to poor Paul. Colin was in Europe at the time, and Solange was pregnant. There was an outbreak of scarlet fever," Mardi explained, noting Wyeth's look of disbelief. "Yes, I know it's hard to believe that people still don't get shots for their children, but like many backwoodspeople anywhere, not all our people believe in them. Anyway, Émile, who practices here and in Montreal, was run ragged. To be on the safe side, Solange was packed off to Montreal, and that devil Amalie made herself available to Émile. Oh, it died a quick death, but not before Amalie made sure that Solange knew in detail of her husband's defection. Their marriage is very strong now, but Solange has not forgotten."

"I should think not," Wyeth murmured, thinking how hurt she had been when Colin was in the other woman's company, knowing she would be torn apart if Colin were married to her and he took up with Amalie. *It's a good thing we're not married,* she told herself morosely.

Wyeth was glad of the demands the children made on Colin throughout the lunch hour. It kept his attention from her.

"Colin, how are the plans coming for the Winter Carnival?" Mardi asked, rescuing Nate's napkin from his plate for the second time. Nate had a ring of peanut butter around his mouth, making Wyeth laugh. "Wouldn't you think he would develop more refined tastes?" his mother sighed. "Kyle says the chef has threatened to quit if he is called upon to look at another peanut butter sandwich."

"Oh, does it bother him to make them?" Wyeth asked.

"Make them?" the others chorused as they looked at Wyeth as though she had taken leave of her senses.

"The great René would never deign to make a sandwich, *ma belle.*" Colin laughed at her comical expression. "There are his staff members that would do that: those at the lowest rung on the ladder would make a peanut butter sandwich, I'm sure." Colin grinned at her. "I remember making sandwiches and having my ear cuffed because the filling was not just so on the bread."

Kyle nodded in grim agreement. "I can remember Marie Clair chasing me around the kitchen with that saber she calls a vegetable knife, saying that she was going to pickle my ears for putting limp lettuce in a sandwich. It was a good thing I was fast on my feet." He smiled at the others in anticipation. "Can you imagine what will happen to Nate when he begins to work in the kitchen?"

The grown-ups looked at the blithely unconcerned Nate as he tried to wad his sandwich into his mouth. His waiter, Jean, wrested it from him and broke him a small piece to eat, not once losing the expressionless look on his face.

Nate looked up at Jean and frowned but chewed the bread anyway.

"He's darling," Wyeth cooed. "Marie Clair will love him."

"God, Wyeth, if you believe that, I'd hate to see how blind you'll be with your own children." Kyle gave her a disgusted look.

"Mine will be perfect," Wyeth predicted.

"Just like me," Colin responded.

"Is this an announcement?" Kyle laughed at the coin-sized red spots on Wyeth's cheeks. "I thought you two weren't even speaking." Kyle put both elbows on the table, put his chin in his hands, and stared at Wyeth. "From all I've heard, Wyeth, from all the brokenhearted women my brother has tossed aside, you'll have a rough time taming him."

"Too rough," Wyeth snapped, glaring at Émile and Mardi. "I don't have the courage to take on the job."

"I'll teach you to be brave, *ma belle*." Colin grinned at her, then raised his coffeecup to the others in salute.

Wyeth fumed while the others laughed.

CHAPTER SEVEN

After lunch Wyeth excused herself by saying that she had to help Mardi put the children down for a nap. When the other woman was about to say something, Wyeth glared at her and lifted Nate into her arms, sleepiness making him limp as a wet noodle.

"I'll see you later, darling," Colin smiled into her glowering face.

"Yes, later." *When we're alone and I can really give you a piece of my mind,* Wyeth steamed to herself, marching ahead of Mardi in stiff-legged resentment. Where did he get off calling her darling after the way he had treated her! She squeezed Nate in reaction, and he muttered a protest. "Sorry, darling, Auntie Wyeth didn't mean it." She helped Mardi undress the children in stony silence. When they left the children's bedrooms, Mardi asked her if she would like a cup of coffee.

"No, thank you." Wyeth responded, simmering down some. "I promised Tante Cecile and Mrs. Arbuthnot that I would stop by their house."

"Don't forget to tell Colin where you are," Mardi said impishly.

"I certainly will not," Wyeth flared. "And don't you tell him where I've gone. I mean it, Mardi; and stop that smirking."

"Yessir." Mardi saluted with one hand over her eye. "What if he threatens my life?"

"Tough." Wyeth turned her back on the giggling Mardi and stalked to the door.

134

She went back to her suite and donned heavy clothing, determined that she was going to avoid Colin.

By the time she reached the ski shop where Beau was in the care of the taciturn Albert, she had cooled down. Still, she was not going to allow Colin to move into her life again so easily—not after the heavy-handed way he had treated her. She only had to think of him with the exotic Amalie on the day of the stockholders' meeting and she started to grind her teeth.

"Hello, Albert," Wyeth greeted the grizzled man with the ever present pipe in his mouth, while trying to fend off the ecstatic greeting of the wriggling Beau.

"*Bonjour, madame,*" he cackled as Beau drove her toward the wall with his affections. "That one is strong, madame." He gestured to the dog with his pipe. "I think he is too strong for you to keep, *hein*?"

"Not at all, Albert." Wyeth defended the now seated dog, panting at her side. "Don't you think his manners improve every day?"

His shrug didn't agree or disagree.

"Albert, may I have some snowshoes please?" Wyeth pointed to the equipment suspended from the ceiling behind the counter.

"No, madame. Monsieur Colin does not want you to go out in the cold without him," he pronounced, sucking on his pipe.

"That's silly, Albert. I'm not going on a trek. I'm just going to walk down the track next to the drive. I'll be back in half an hour. I just want to get some fresh air, to relax."

"Ah, *oui*, I have heard what you did with *le petit*, madame. It was good. Can you not relax in your room?"

Wyeth pleaded for many more minutes before the phlegmatic Albert could be convinced that she wouldn't leave the grounds just surrounding the château.

Finally, with Albert's assurances that he would come looking for her if she was not back in allotted time, she left with Beau on a leash.

"He treats me like a baby, Beau. Is that fair?" Wyeth muttered to the dog as she struggled to master the frying-pan shaped fittings on her boots.

After a few moments she developed a slow rhythm that carried her forward in a steady way. Beau gamboled left and right, reveling in the deep snow.

"Dammit, woman, don't you listen to anyone," Colin shouted just behind them.

Wyeth swiveled her body so that she could watch the way he ran with ease in the clumsy snowshoes. The swiveling put her out of balance, and she sank into a snowbank. "Damn you, Colin. I was doing just fine until you yelled at me," she sputtered, her gloved hand wiping the snow from her face. Beau was all over her, making it virtually impossible for her to rise.

Instead of helping Colin put his hands on his hips and laughed down at her. "Serves you right for not listening to Albert. I chewed him out good for letting you come without me."

"That was high-handed of you," Wyeth sputtered, managing at last to extricate herself from the dog and stagger to her feet. "A gentleman would have helped me to rise."

"If you insist on coming out alone, you had better learn to pull yourself erect," he snarled, reaching for her two elbows and lifting her close to his body. "I missed you like hell, Wyeth."

His mouth felt like a satin ram forcing hers to open. The heat from his body threaded through hers, making her body feel instantly molten and melded with his.

God, I hate this power he has over me, Wyeth thought in dazed anger. *How can I let myself be so completely taken over?* She moaned to herself while her arms were twining round his body, hugging him to her.

"Don't ever make me that angry again with you. I hate it," he mumbled against her mouth.

"Me?" Wyeth croaked. "It wasn't me. It was you and that Dragon Lady aunt of yours."

"Don't be a fool," Colin's mouth teased her, back and forth.

136

"I'm not the fool," Wyeth squeaked, feeling her toes wriggle in reaction to Colin's touch.

"Let's go to bed," Colin demanded.

"I can't," Wyeth wailed. "I have to see Tante Cecile in fifteen minutes."

"Cancel it."

"No. You're too bossy," Wyeth rallied, trying to free herself from his grasp. "I'm going to see Tante because I promised, and I'm going to walk Beau. He needs the exercise."

"And I need you." Colin glared down at her, pulling her closer. "I should be your first priority."

Wyeth gasped. "Of all the pompous, egotistical, bossy—"

Colin leaned down and covered her mouth with his again, branding her with his touch, his assertive tongue possessing hers. "You're mine. All the name-calling in the world doesn't change that," he said, his own breathing unsteady. He put a finger to her lips, stopping her sputters. "All right, this time we do it your way; but don't think that's the way it will be all the time. It won't." He turned and whistled to Beau, who earned Wyeth's curses by coming at once.

It was fun to do anything with Colin, Wyeth admitted to herself as she watched him throw snowballs for the intrigued Beau. Beau had no retriever in him. He evinced that time and time again as he pounced on the snowball and mangled it out of shape.

When Colin ran back to her, his face was reddened with cold, his beard flecked with snow, his eyes emerald bright. To Wyeth he looked healthy, virile, and very dangerous, but she indulged herself by staring at him and drinking in his looks.

"What are you thinking, *ma belle*?" He touched her cold cheek with an ungloved finger. "You looked forlorn for a moment. Are you tired?"

"Tired? Me?" Wyeth smiled at him, then backed away and scooped up some snow. "I'll show you who's tired." She flung the snow even as she spoke.

Colin's quick reflexes permitted him to duck most of it, but some caught him high on his right cheek, spraying his beard.

Wyeth laughed and turned to run. Colin's tackle brought her down in a snowbank, his own body cushioning hers, so that she didn't hit hard. She tried to cover herself, laughing all the while, Beau barking beside them. She pleaded with him not to wash her face in the snow.

"All right, I'll let you off this time. Kiss me instead," he demanded, pulling her down to lie on top of him.

"Oh, that's a fate worse than getting my face washed in snow," Wyeth giggled, then ducked her face under his chin.

"Kiss me, Wyeth."

"Brute." She smiled, then placed her mouth at the corner of his, slowly moving her lips across his, liking the role of aggressor.

"Wyeth, don't tease."

"Am I teasing?" She didn't allow him to respond, but instead pressed her mouth, inhaling his words into her own mouth. Wyeth had no idea how long they lay there next to the path, bedded in the snowbank, but she became irritated when he shifted and began lifting her from his body.

"I refuse to take you in the snow, *ma belle*. You'd catch cold." Colin was smiling, but his lips were unsteady.

"You have no sense of adventure," Wyeth chided, trying to keep her voice light, but not succeeding.

"I'll give you all the adventure you wish when we're back in your suite." He lifted her to her feet and dusted the snow from her. "And tonight, darling, I'm sleeping in your bedroom," he threatened, watching for her reaction, girding himself for battle.

Wyeth didn't say anything at first, letting another couple with cross-country skis on pass them on the path. "Colin, why were you so angry with me on the day of the stockholders' meeting? Why didn't you talk to me?"

"Because I was afraid that I'd blow my top and drive you away from me. As angry as I was with you, I didn't want to do that," he said, grim tones bracketing his mouth.

138

"But why did you get angry?"

"Because you were with Luc." He bit the word in half like bitter fruit. "Because he was holding you."

"Colin, Luc means nothing to me." Wyeth couldn't hide the pleasure she felt because of Colin's jealousy.

"He damn well better not, and don't you smile about it either, Wyeth. It's not funny. I won't have him hanging around you." His chin thrusting forward reminded Wyeth of little Nate.

She refused to be mollified. After all, there was Amalie.

"And am I supposed to twiddle my thumbs while you carry on behind my back?"

"Me, carry on? With whom?" Colin looked dumbfounded.

"What an actor you are!" Wyeth snapped. "Amalie as much as told me that you and she were marrying."

"I am not marrying Amalie." Colin spoke in measured tones. "We had a thing going in college for a while, but that was over years ago. She married my cousin Paul after we broke up. There's nothing between us now."

Wyeth looked at him and believed him, but wished that he wasn't so casual about Amalie. She was sure the woman meant to have Colin using any trick in the book. Somehow Wyeth couldn't say this to him. She sighed. "I do have to get back. I'm late for my appointment with Tante."

"All right. I'll let you go, but promise me you'll go to see Émile when you're through. I want him to look at you."

"Why?" Wyeth laughed. "I'm fine. I just feel a little under the weather now and then, but the doctors said that I might."

"Please."

"All right." She nodded. "I'll call him and make an appointment to see him."

They stood embracing outside the ski shop until Albert coughed.

"Monsieur Colin, you wish to have the people of Montbel thinking you a stag panting for his mate?" Albert said this in French, but Colin translated, laughing.

When Wyeth glared at Albert, he shrugged, knocking the dottle from his pipe by striking it against his boot.

"Shall we have dinner together in your suite?" Colin brushed his lips across hers, ignoring Albert's snort of amusement.

"I promised your brother and Mardi I would dine with them tonight so that we could discuss the decorations for the Winter Ball and Carnival." Wyeth answered, alternately smiling at Colin and glowering at Albert who watched them with mild interest.

"Cancel it."

"Oh, Colin, I promised." She looked down at her watch and gasped. "I'm late, and I have to shower. I'll talk to you later."

Wyeth galloped for the elevator, another of Albert's dry comments making Colin laugh. Wyeth promised herself that she would roll the ubiquitous Albert down the slopes of Montbel the very first chance she had.

She accomplished her shower and dressing in mere minutes, donning the denim outfit she had worn for her first interview with Colin. She smiled in memory as she dressed in the sheepskin jacket Colin had given her and slipped on fleece-lined walking boots for the short walk to Tante Cecile's house, which was on a pine-dotted hillock overlooking the Ottawa River not far from the château, but very private.

Wyeth saw the sleigh outside the log-sided chalet that one of the sons of Marie Clair used to bring Tante to the château for dinner. Colin had told her that it had a removable top, which was attached when it was snowing and protected Tante from the elements. Colin had laughed when he told her that not one citizen of Montbel would allow a snowflake to touch Tante if there was anything they could do to prevent it.

Wyeth mounted the wooden steps leading to the front door, eager to see and chat with the live-wired lady who held sway over Montbel.

Mrs. Arbuthnot greeted her with a kiss and led her toward the main room.

Wyeth froze in the doorway when she saw Amalie lounging near the fire, opposite Tante, who turned to smile at Wyeth.

"Come in, child. I was telling Amalie that we intended to have a nice long chat, but . . ." Tante turned to frown at Amalie. "Didn't I tell you that Wyeth was coming to visit me this afternoon and that we wanted to have a long talk, just the two of us?"

"How could I remember all the things you tell me, Tante? There are so many." Amalie smiled, but the eyes that looked at Wyeth were hard. "Well, don't just stand there, Wyeth, do come in. You are keeping poor Mrs. Arbuthnot standing all this time."

Wyeth moved forward, fighting the temper that Amalie's words brought to the surface and the feeling of gaucherie that the other woman was aware of, Wyeth was sure. "Would it be better if I came another time, Tante Cecile?" Wyeth quizzed, sitting next to the older woman on the needlepointed settee.

"*Non, non, ma petite.* I want you here. In your honor I am having tea, which I loathe, because I hear you drink enough of the stuff to be English." Tante shivered, making Wyeth laugh.

"I do. It was a habit I picked up in law school when I found that coffee made me jumpy. I switched to tea and have been drinking it ever since."

"Colin would never stand for that. He likes coffee in the French way." Amalie leaned forward and poured some of the thick brew into her own cup, a curl to her lip.

"I don't think that it's Wyeth's tea-drinking or lack of it that interests Colin," Tante Cecile observed, her tones dry.

Amalie shot a baleful glance at Mrs. Arbuthnot as the woman tittered, then pressed fingers to her mouth. "No, of course; you are right, Tante. It's Wyeth's shares in Montbel that pull his attention."

"I didn't mean that, Amalie," Tante snapped, dropping three cubes of sugar into her tea with angry clicks of the silver tongs.

"No, of course, you are too kind," Amalie soothed, the glitter in her eyes making Wyeth's temper heat like an active volcano.

"I'll admit that Colin's interests in me are quite basic," Wyeth interjected, her voice smooth. "Perhaps earthy would be a more apt word." Her smile rested on Amalie for a moment before turning back to Tante, then to Mrs. Arbuthnot. Tante's cackle and Amalie's gasp seemed to goad her, and she took a deep breath. "Mrs. Arbuthnot, Colin tells me that you are instrumental in introducing some very succulent desserts to Montbel that are not French." Wyeth was very aware that Amalie had been in direct opposition to such a move. She knew that the gleam of amusement in Mrs. Arbuthnot's eyes acknowledged the hit, since Colin had wholeheartedly endorsed the move for the new dessert cart, preferred along with the traditional tray of French pastries.

"Yes," Tante answered. "And they are doing well. We get what you Americans call 'foodback' on this, good 'foodback.'"

Wyeth looked puzzled.

"I think you mean feedback, Cecile," Mrs. Arbuthnot corrected.

Tante shrugged. "Yes, that must be it. Americans talk so strangely, not even English."

Wyeth laughed. "I had a professor in college who agrees with you."

Tante turned to Wyeth, her eyes piercing. "Are you going to marry my Colin?"

Wyeth choked. Mrs. Arbuthnot protested. Only Amalie spoke.

"I doubt whether Wyeth would want to marry Colin, Tante. I am sure she would feel it was tragic to bring the taint of her family to another member of the MacLendons and the Colberts." Amalie toyed with her cup, her lashes masking the look she gave Wyeth.

Tante was glaring at Amalie. Mrs. Arbuthnot was frowning at her. Neither woman noticed that Wyeth had whitened, that the hand holding the tea was shaking. She felt her blood pounding in her head and silently prayed that she wouldn't faint.

"What are you saying, Amalie?" Tante snapped, banging her stick on the floor. "What foolishness is this?"

Amalie shrugged, a placating smile on her lips. "Well, Tante, it seems there are those who consider Wyeth—how shall I say it—an unlucky person, and would not want her to marry into our family a—"

"Nonsense, Amalie," Mrs. Arbuthnot interjected. "You are not a superstitious person. Why do you talk this way?"

"Fustian, pure fustian," Tante said, disapproval in every line of her body. "I will not have such talk, do you hear me Amalie?"

"Whatever you say, Tante," Amalie answered, a smile playing around her lips, her eyes darting to Wyeth's face.

Wyeth truly appreciated the fact that Tante Cecile dismissed the notion as utter nonsense. But to Wyeth the damage had already been done. Her head throbbed, and her heart ached. She longed to be with Colin, to feel the comfort of his strong embrace blocking out these irrational, painful thoughts. But how long would they continue to be happy before something awful happened? Oh Lord, she thought suddenly, can I possibly be thinking that it's true?

The rest of the visit was a haze to Wyeth. She tried to respond at the proper time, concentrating on keeping her face composed, aware that if she wasn't vigilant, she would crumple weeping on the carpet.

When she rose to leave, Amalie rose with her. Wyeth was unable to prevent the other woman from accompanying her.

When the path took a bend through the trees, out of sight of Tante's chalet, Wyeth swung to face the other woman. "Amalie, I think we'll part here. You and I have nothing to say to each other, and I'm sure my company is just as distasteful to you as yours is to me." Wyeth's mouth felt frozen, the effort to speak almost overpowering.

"Since there is just this path back to the château, you will have to bear with me. I will not walk through the brush."

Without another word Wyeth spun on her heel and began to

trot down the path. This was no easy task since there were patches of ice on the path, but she didn't care. All that mattered was putting distance between herself and the other woman. Wyeth had the feeling that if she had stayed, she would have punched Amalie in the eye.

She rounded another bend and slid right against Colin's chest.

"Whoa. Take it slower, Wyeth." Colin laughed down at her, then lifted her up against his chest, her feet dangling in the heavy boots. "I missed you, too, darling, so I came to fetch you."

His kiss was a soothing balm to her lacerated spirit. For a moment all Wyeth did was hang there, letting him oil her ruffled senses. Then his tongue probed hers, the ever present embers of passion flaring to life between them.

"Well, Colin, have you come to see Wyeth and me back to the château?" Amalie's voice was low, but Wyeth could hear the thread of anger there.

She didn't turn to look at the other woman but watched Colin's frown as he lowered Wyeth to the ground, though he didn't release her from his arms.

"What are you doing here, Amalie? Wyeth didn't tell me you were joining her at Tante's."

"She didn't know. I just happened to drop by to see Tante; then Wyeth arrived," Amalie explained, her fingers latching onto his arm. "I hope we're not going to stand here in the cold discussing this. I'm dying for a hot rum punch. Will you make it for me, Colin?"

"If I have time after Wyeth and I are dressed," Colin said.

"Oh, no, that's too late. Make it before I go to change for dinner, or I won't be able to move. You know how cramped I get from the cold, Colin."

"Have Luc make it then, Amalie. I have to get Wyeth into the sauna for a while. She hasn't been well, you know."

"Oh, are you convinced of that?" Amalie quizzed.

Colin laughed as Wyeth glared at the other woman. "Amalie, I have always given you credit for shrewdness, but if you contin-

144

ue to bait Wyeth, I'll have to assume you're stupid. My little tiger here is apt to knock you on your derriere if you make her mad enough." He laughed again when Wyeth glared at him.

Amalie said no more, but the look she gave Wyeth when Colin hugged her to his side would have melted steel.

When they were in Wyeth's room, Colin insisted on stripping off her things, then leading her to the small sauna that was installed in the bathroom.

Wyeth couldn't help the vein of pleasure that ran through her as she looked at Colin stretched out beside her.

"I like the way you look at me, *ma belle*. You know, before you came to Montbel, I rarely used this facility, but since your arrival, I have come to love saunas." He grinned at her, his strong hands massaging oil into her back while she sat there.

"I like the sauna," Wyeth said, her words sounding stilted to her ears. She was reeling from the sensations that Colin was evoking from her body. "Shall—shall I massage you now, Colin?" Wyeth asked, her voice sounding reedy.

"Ummm, you know I love to have you touch me, *petite;* even when you claw me, it is better than another woman's stroking."

"And you have had so many women to compare me to," she replied, the sudden asperity in her voice making Colin smile.

"*Mais oui, amour,* I admit it. Would you have me an untried celibate at the ripe old age of thirty-six?" he crooned to her, his mouth feathering her shoulder.

Wyeth stiffened at his laughter, jerking her shoulder away from him and gripping the oil flask in her hand. "No. I didn't expect you to be celibate, but I didn't expect you to be a *sultan*, either."

His deep laughter as he turned his back to her made her teeth grind together.

Her first strokes on his back were rough, but he didn't say anything. Without Wyeth's conscious wish the strokes became gentler, more soothing.

"Yes, love, that's better," Colin whispered, turning to take her in his arms.

She let one long, sharp nail rake down his chest, the thin red line not breaking the skin. "With just a little pressure, I could give you an interesting scar," Wyeth murmured, her eyes following the trail of her finger.

"Angry with me, darling?" he queried, letting his hand graze her breast in gentle questing.

"Yes, damn you." Wyeth couldn't hold back a smile. "How dare you sleep with other women!" She pulled the chestnut hairs on his chest, plucking at them with a fierceness that made him wince. Yet he made no move to stop her.

"And damn you for marrying Nate. I hated Nate. Did you know that?" His lips twisted in a semblance of a smile. "When I found that you had been married to him, I suddenly forgot every kind thought I'd ever had about the man." He grasped her hand and turned his mouth into the palm. "Crazy, isn't it?"

"Yes," she answered, her voice unsteady. "I shall take your cousin Amalie apart in bite-size pieces and feed her to one of Beau's relatives," Wyeth said, her voice tart.

"Tiger," Colin laughed, nuzzling his face into her breasts. "I suspect I would be in real trouble if I were ever unfaithful." He slid down her abdomen.

"I'd dismember you." Wyeth gasped as he took hold of her body and let her slip through his hands.

"In that case, I'll behave," Colin breathed, his voice distracted. "Would you believe that I would never risk losing you?"

"I make it a policy never to believe what a handsome man tells me." Wyeth nibbled at his ear as he led her to the shower, his arm hugging her tightly to his side.

"Do you think I'm handsome, Wyeth?" Colin queried as he fumbled with the shower head and switched on the water. "It's funny, *petite,* I never gave a damn what women thought of me—my looks, my mind, anything. Now I want to know."

"I think . . . you're passable." Wyeth laughed, provoking the retaliation she knew would come. She took the other Loofa sponge from the soap caddy and lathered it with a fragrant liquid essence that Colin had purchased for her in Montreal.

"My God, Wyeth, what are you doing? I won't be able to go into the dining room smelling like that."

"I don't care. You smell gorgeous." She giggled as they stepped out of the shower and he began to dry her, careful to pat softly around the reddened scar tissue.

"You are getting better, *ma belle*. There is much less swelling." He kissed her hip, then stood up and hugged her close. "God, Wyeth, do you realize how frightened I was when I saw you on that three-meter board."

"I felt you beside me as soon as I hit," she crooned, pulling his head down to her. "I had no fear then."

"Wyeth, darling, you're a part of me now," he groaned, his body tensing as she stroked him.

For a moment he looked down at her, his eyes touching every feature, then his mouth closed over hers.

Nothing mattered but the desperate need that flared between them.

Wyeth's hand lifted as though in mute answer to an order and caressed his body, seeming to know at once what would please Colin just as his touch inflamed her. She couldn't get enough of him, as though she had been denied air to breathe and it was suddenly given back to her. She gave herself over to him totally, joyfully. There was no holding back for either of them.

As Colin again pursued and persuaded, his touch sent warm rivers of pleasure through every inch of her being. Wyeth felt herself out of control as he led and coaxed her to an even greater fulfillment than she had experienced the other times they had made love. Along the way his own pleasure mounted as Wyeth fondled him with her hands and her mouth.

Their coming-together was violent but peaceful, thunderous but silent, as they gripped each other in ecstatic release.

"Darling, don't fall asleep," Wyeth mumbled, her own eyelids fluttering.

"Just for a few minutes," Colin muttered, tucking her close to his body. " 'Sfunny, but I don't sleep as well anymore when you're not with me." He yawned so wide, his jaw cracked; then he was asleep.

Wyeth argued with herself whether to stay awake, not wanting to be late. The family was coming this evening en masse to hear the plans for the Winter Carnival.

The gentle shaking irritated her. She woke with a frown on her face to see Colin laughing down at her. Her answering smile was reluctant and wondering. "Hello." She swallowed thickly.

"Hello." He grinned, lifting her from the bed and carrying her to the bathroom. "It's a wake-up shower for you, lady, and a very quick one at that. Dinner is in ten minutes."

Wyeth squealed at the rush of water and the time. "Oh, Colin, I'll never make it."

"Yes, we will," he promised as he massaged her body with the Loofa in quick strokes, contenting himself with tiny kisses. Then he was lifting her out of the shower and wrapping her in a bath sheet before swathing himself in one as well.

Wyeth wailed at the mess as Colin layered her in clouds of talc. "What will Marie say?"

"She'll have to tough it out this once. She knows that we're generally neater. Come along, love; I laid out that white thing with all the pleats. It makes you look like a bride." Colin smiled at her, his eyes warm.

Wyeth felt her heart contract in pain. He couldn't be thinking that way! He mustn't spoil things. She was firm in her mind that she would not marry him, just in case she was a jinx. . . . No, she wouldn't think like that.

"What is it, darling? You look blue." Colin looked over her shoulder while tying the black silk bow tie that complemented his evening clothes. "Are you feeling all right? Mardi said that you were feeling headachy and—"

"Don't be silly, Colin." She smiled at him in the mirror. "I told you the doctors told me that I would have times like that. It's something to do with the medication, plus the healing. It's nothing. I pay no attention to it. By midmorning I'm fine."

He didn't look convinced, but he didn't say any more about it. Instead, while she was still sitting in front of the dressing table putting the finishing touches to her toilette and just before she reached for her jewel case, he handed her a green-velvet jewel case that Wyeth could tell was quite old. "Open it, darling. They're for you. They belonged to my mother."

"Colin, I can't," she began, but he leaned over her, his mouth just covering hers, taking care not to smear her lip gloss.

"You must. They belong to you. Open it," he insisted, an expectant glitter to his eyes.

Wyeth gasped at the prismatic flash of the diamonds that laid curled on the white-satin interior. A baguette diamond necklace was matched with baguette teardrop earrings.

"A beautiful woman should only be adorned with the finest jewels, *petite*," Colin whispered, lifting the necklace and placing it around her neck, then clasping it. The cream-colored pleated dress that fell from under her breasts in an uneven fall seemed to take on all the colors thrown off by the diamonds.

"Oh, Colin," she gasped; too moved to even thank him properly, she flung her arms around his neck and hugged him tight.

Wyeth's hands were shaking as she fitted the earrings to her ears, then stared at the now sophisticated woman, her long neck emphasized by the richness of the stones.

"Darling, I'd love to let you gape at yourself for hours, but we're already twenty minutes late for dinner." Colin laughed as Wyeth jumped to her feet and galloped to the door. "*Ma belle*, you don't look the grand lady of Montbel—more like a child who is in trouble with the headmistress."

"Never mind that. Hurry. You know Tante will scold you." She glared at him.

"She loves you, Wyeth. She won't say anything," Colin assured her as he took her arm to go down the main stairway to the dining room.

"But the rest of them . . . they'll be looking. They'll think— well, you know," Wyeth muttered, holding back as they approached the alcove where the family gathered.

"They'll think we've been making love," Colin laughed in her ear, making her redden.

"Shhhh," Wyeth begged, as an army of heads turned their way.

Solange and Mardi appeared complacent as they looked across Émile's chest at each other. Émile's grin was echoed by Kyle's, and Wyeth wanted to hit the two of them.

She was glad of the distraction when Colin introduced her to an array of cousins who, he explained, had arrived to help with the Winter Carnival. Wyeth didn't even try to remember their names.

"Wyeth," Mardi caroled. "You're wearing Mother MacLendon's diamonds. How lovely they look on you," she simpered, looking over at Amalie. "I have her sapphires, and Solange has the pearls."

"How nice," Wyeth managed, grateful to be sitting between Colin and Bill Balmain.

"I think Mardi is trying to tell you that Colin in his subtle way has made an announcement." Bill smiled at her.

"No," Wyeth said in dawning horror, her hand going in slow motion to the necklace. "It doesn't mean that," she whispered, but no one seemed to be listening. As usual, the MacLendons and the Colberts were talking to each other in uninterrupted cadence. The plans for the Carnival seemed to take preference, but a myriad of other topics were covered as well. Wyeth's panicky feeling began to subside. She was even able to smile at Émile and nod yes that she would visit him on the following morning. She felt taken up by the thrust of the conversation and carried away. She did not once look toward the table where Amalie and Luc were sitting.

"Colin insisted that I allow Nate and Annette to visit us for dessert, Wyeth." Mardi leaned across the table, her eyebrows raising at the thought. "God knows what will happen."

Wyeth laughed, looking forward to seeing the two children.

As the dessert cart was being taken away the baby-sitter guided the children down the stairs. From his height in the baby-sitter's arms Nate spotted Wyeth.

"*Y, Y, Y, Y, Y,*" he roared, making the other diners guffaw and his mother wince.

"Here I am, darling." Wyeth rose to take him and turned. The movement caused her a momentary dizziness. She put her hand to her head.

Colin stood at once. "What is it, *ma belle*?"

"Nothing. I just moved too fast after eating, I think."

Émile was at her other side. "Do you have these spells often?"

"No."

"She had one at my place one morning," Mardi said, taking Nate from Wyeth, shushing him when he began to howl.

Wyeth returned to her chair and held her arms up to Nate. "Let me take him, Mardi. I'll just hold him in my lap."

"Émile, I would like you to examine her tonight," Colin ordered, his voice rough.

Before Émile could answer, Wyeth reached up and pulled Colin's arm. "Don't be silly. Sit down please. I explained about the dizziness."

"But you should not have it this long, Wyeth." Émile spoke, his voice dry, accepting a cheroot from Colin and rolling it between his fingers. "Ah, don't look so dismayed, *chérie*. I will not examine you tonight. Time enough tomorrow."

Colin stared at his brother-in-law, narrowed-eyed.

"And don't you look at my husband as though you wish to kill him, *cher frère*," Solange prodded her brother. "Let him be the doctor."

"Might we adjourn to the sitting room and have coffee?"

151

Amalie interjected. "How can we possibly plan the Carnival if we are going to be sidestepped by minutiae?"

Solange swelled with indignation. As she rose to her feet to do battle Tante Cecile tapped her on the wrist.

"Come. Amalie is right. We will have coffee in the sitting room. Solange, let me take your arm. Mardi, you will walk on my other side. Colin and Kyle will bring the children."

In fact, it was Bill Balmain who carried Nate, with Wyeth walking behind them so that Nate could see her. Annette was with her Uncle Colin.

When they settled in informal fashion in the sitting room, Tante was first to speak. "In other years we have had one of the family members open the Carnival, usually one of the men. This year I think we should change that and let the women open it. I think Solange and Mardi are the logical ones to do this. Does anyone object to this?" she asked, her voice severe.

Wyeth could see that Amalie objected, but she refrained from saying anything.

"Wyeth, did you know that Bill has signed you up to play as his partner in the curling contest?" Mardi giggled.

Wyeth swiveled her head to look at Bill.

He nodded. "Guilty. We'll win. With your beauty and my brawn we'll be unbeatable."

Wyeth laughed along with the rest, but protested that she knew nothing of the game. "I only played once with Colin, and I was bad, wasn't I?" She looked at Colin, but he was staring down into his drink, his expression a stern mask, white lines pinching his mouth.

"I think we have better things to do than discuss the merits of curling." He spat the words, bringing the attention of the others to him.

CHAPTER EIGHT

Colin was not speaking to her again. Well, Wyeth amended to herself, he was growling at her, but that could hardly be called speaking. *She* had no intention of responding to his black mood. How dare he treat her so coldly in front of the family! Who did he think he was? she muttered to herself as she applied talcum powder to her body after bathing and readied herself for her appointment with Émile. She glared at the green-velvet jewel case that housed the MacLendon diamonds. They were going back to Colin's room this morning. In the meantime she placed them in the small wall safe that Colin had shown her how to use. It was hidden behind the full-length mirror attached to the wall near the dressing room. Wyeth closed the mirror with a decisive snap and took a deep breath. Now to see Émile.

The examination was quite thorough. Wyeth was at the point of asking Émile if all of it was necessary, but each time she tried to broach the question, he disarmed her with a smile and a platitude. Wyeth submitted to the lengthy examination with a sigh, wishing she was through with doctors, happy that she had only one final operation to face and, at that, a small one only, to clean off some of the scar tissue.

When she was finally dressed, she joined Émile in his office, relaxing in the chair that he had arranged in front of his desk. He leaned forward on the pyramid of his hands, smiling at her. She smiled back, knowing, because of his impish grin, that he had nothing disastrous to tell her.

"I must be in excellent health if your smile is any gauge." Wyeth settled herself more deeply into the overstuffed leather chair, her hands held loosely in her lap.

"Well . . ." The Gallic shrug was there. "I would rather you had put it off to some future time when all your surgical procedures were at an end, but I would say that it looks good." He nodded to her, shifting some prescription slips forward on his desk. He lifted his half-glasses back onto his nose. "Now, this is a vitamin therapy that I would like you to be on. This could be changed by Étienne, I suppose, but for now—"

"Étienne? Who is Étienne?" she asked Émile, a puzzled look on her face.

"Étienne Aubert. He was a classmate of mine at McGill. He's very good. I sent Solange and Mardi to him. Of course, you are open to choose anyone, and there are others I can recommend, but I think— What is it, Wyeth? Why are you looking at me that way?"

"What are you saying, Émile?" she quizzed in fading accents.

Émile rose from behind his desk, throwing down his glasses. "Wyeth, didn't you know you were pregnant?" He knelt next to her chair, taking one of her hands in his.

She shook her head in a measured motion. "I can't be. The doctors said that I might never have children because of the accident."

"Doctors can be wrong. Didn't you notice that you hadn't menstruated?"

"Yes, but that wasn't unusual. I have often missed periods since the accident. I didn't think anything of it."

Émile stroked her hand, smiling at her. "Well, I judge you to be about two months along, Wyeth. I see no abnormality or foresee any problem. Of course, we will have to watch your blood since you were so anemic there for a while. Right now you are not. You are still too thin, but you are in quite good health."

"And the baby will be fine?" She turned her head to look at

154

Émile, a look of awe on her face.

"I see no reason why you shouldn't have a beautiful baby. Have you not noticed that your clothes are getting tighter?"

"Yes," Wyeth reddened. "I just thought it was regular weight gain and was glad that I was coming along so fast."

"Well, you sure are coming along," Émile laughed, kissing her cheek and rising to his feet. He headed for his chair. "Colin will be pleased."

Wyeth started forward in her chair. "No. Colin mustn't know, Émile. Please."

Émile frowned, lifting her folder in two hands, two spots of red high on his cheeks. "I have been gauche. Colin is not the father?"

"Yes, of course he is." Wyeth gave him an irritated look.

He let his breath go in a whistle. "I'm glad to hear that. I would not want to be around Colin if he even thought that it wasn't his child."

"He is not to be told, Émile," she stated, her tones firm. "I mean that."

"Why? Am I permitted to ask that question?" Émile had an angry glint to his eye. "He's the father. He has a right to know. Besides which, he will destroy me and his sister will help him if I keep such a secret."

"Please, Émile, you must keep this confidential until after I leave Montbel. I intend to raise my baby alone. Give me your word you will say nothing."

"It is not necessary. There is the patient/doctor code of confidentiality," he said stiffly. "I would not say anything anyway. I would leave that up to you. I urge you not to keep this from Colin, Wyeth. It's wrong."

"No, it's not wrong. He does not want to be saddled with marriage. He would feel it was his duty to marry me if he found out. I don't want that. It's my fault that no preventive measures were taken, not Colin's."

"There is always abortion," Émile said, his lips compressed.

"No." Wyeth smiled. "I want this baby. I'm happy to be pregnant. I'll be leaving Montbel, and I'll raise the child elsewhere. I have a home in another city."

"When will you leave Montbel?" Émile asked, his face sad.

Wyeth took a deep breath and looked out the window. It wouldn't be easy to leave this lovely place. "I'll go after the Winter Carnival. I want to be here for that." She turned back to look at Émile, a shimmer of tears in her eyes. "I'll miss everyone here more than I can say, but I know I'm doing the right thing for the baby . . . for everyone."

"I do not agree, but I will help you all I can." Émile rose to his feet, then came round his desk to sit on the corner of it. "What am I to say to Colin when he asks me about you? And you can be sure he will ask me. He is like a mother hen about you."

"Tell him the truth. Tell him I'm in good shape and getting better," Wyeth answered, her smile not quite steady.

When Wyeth returned to her room, she found that her hands were shaking, her body covered with a thin film of perspiration. She was going to have a baby! she thought, studying her naked form in the full-length mirror in the bathroom. She would have something of Colin forever. Tears coursed down her cheeks as she stared at her mirror image. How she would care for this baby!

She was leaning over the tub adjusting the water, when the door pushed open behind her. Wyeth didn't turn around, thinking it was Marie coming to scold her because she hadn't rung to have Marie prepare the bath. "Now, Marie, before you say anything, let me tell you that I am perfectly capable of running my own bath. I am sure Monsieur Colin does not expect you to fuss over me."

"Oh, yes he does expect you to be fussed over," Colin laughed behind her, running his hands over her hips, leaning over her as he usually did to kiss the scar on her hip. "In fact, at this moment

156

he is going to join you in the bath while you tell what Émile said to you."

"Have you talked to Émile?" Wyeth hedged, stepping to one side as Colin began to pour oils into the water. "Oh, Colin, not so much. I'll slide all over the place, and I won't be able to find my way through the bubbles." Wyeth looked in alarm at the rising volcano of froth.

"It will relax you," he insisted, putting the bottles aside, then helping Wyeth down into the bubbles, grinning when she waved the stuff away from her face. "Of course, I've spoken to Émile. He called me the minute you left his office, on my instructions." He dropped the last of his clothing in careless disarray.

Wyeth felt dry-mouthed as she looked at the bronzed strength of him. "I've been meaning to ask you how you managed that allover tan of yours."

He let that lazy look pinpoint her face. "I usually take a vacation on a little island I have near St. Thomas. It's very private. When I take you there, you'll get a nice allover tan, too, *ma belle.*" He grinned when he saw the tinge of red in her cheeks. "Sometimes I use a sunlamp, but not often. The damn things bore me. Move over, *ma mie.* I'm joining you."

Wyeth squealed as Colin lowered himself into the tub, closing her mind to the time when she would be parted from him. Time enough to brood on that when she was alone. Now she gave herself up to the enjoyment of the man who had become the center of her life.

She allowed her fingers to run up the smoothness of his back, smiling at his look of surprise as she became the aggressor.

"You are a constant surprise to me, *ma belle,*" Colin whispered, his voice hoarse, his body clenching as her hands roved over him. A raw look spread over his features as Wyeth's ministrations increased, as he tried to fight the grip of sensation. "God, Wyeth. You're pulling me to pieces." He pulled her water-slick body over his own, the sliding action firming him even more. The hands that feathered Wyeth's body shook. "You're mine, Wyeth." He lifted his head back a fraction to study her bubbled, speckled face. "Say you're mine, *ma mie,* say it."

"I am yours, Colin," Wyeth breathed, knowing it was true, knowing there would be no other man in her life. Colin had spoiled her for anyone else. With a happy sadness she clutched him tighter.

"And you'll be mine forever?" Colin mumbled, his lips close to her ear.

"As long as I'm at Montbel, I'll be yours," Wyeth said, biting at his chin.

Colin moved her away from him so that he could look at her. "That isn't the answer I wanted." He looked at her in narrow-eyed scrutiny. Then he grinned. "But since you won't be leaving Montbel ever, I can accept that." He rubbed her stomach.

Wyeth had seen a hesitant look appear on his face before he could phrase the question.

She leaned over him letting her mouth rub back and forth on his. She could feel his heart shift into high gear as it lay under her breasts. She reeled with a sense of power as his hands bit into her. She gasped, and the hands relaxed at once, moving over her with a silky possessiveness that told her more than words ever could that he wanted her.

Mouths clinging, bodies entwined, Wyeth had the surrealistic sureness that they were in the middle of an ocean, not a tub, that they were floating away never to return.

"I can't get close enough to you this way, *ma belle,*" Colin growled at her, his body heaving upward, carrying them both to a sitting position before Colin's strong body propelled them to their feet. He balanced them both with feet wide apart.

Wyeth was content for him to call the tune and relaxed with her arms twined around his neck. She blew in his ear, feeling with a sense of urgency that she wanted to touch him in every way. She would store up the memories for the time when she would be alone. She would have much to tell her child about the man who was his father. His? she mused, letting her head loll as Colin dried her hair. It might be a girl. A girl with chestnut-colored hair and deep green eyes. Wyeth smiled to herself.

"What are you thinking, Wyeth?" Colin quizzed her as he lifted her high in his arms. "Are you thinking how easily you caught me?"

"Conceited." She punched his shoulder, then bit his ear. "You were a pushover."

"Pushover, am I?" Colin laughed, placing her on the bed, then leaning over her. "So you admit you set out to trap me."

"Arrogant, bubble-headed man," Wyeth sputtered, trying to sit up, pushing at Colin's restraining arm. "You chased me."

"Not true." Colin shook his head, his eyes alight as he looked at her pugnacious face. "I can't believe what a wonderful person I've been through all this," he muttered as she struggled to hit him and he leaned over a hardening nipple. She heard his deep chuckle when she gasped. He lifted his head from her breast, his eyes glittering. "Such care I've taken of you! I could tell when I carried you from the bath that you'd gained weight. All that good Montbel food is giving you curves again, *ma mie*," he growled, lowering his head again over her breasts.

Slowly Wyeth covered his head with her hands, her body reacting spasmodically to his touch. She was grateful that he wasn't looking at her face, which she knew had reddened at his alluding to her weight.

His laughter rippled over her again when he felt the trembling that she couldn't control. His eyes were a hot liquid green when they lifted from her. "You have a most lovely body, my own. A body that I have to have."

Wyeth tried to answer in a throat gone dry as his body stretched and hardened over hers. "Make love to me, Colin," she sighed.

"I fully intend to, Wyeth; now and for years to come, I'll make

159

love to you." His hoarse vow ignited her, setting every part of her glowing with a liquid fire.

Their lovemaking was like a spiral that drew them into a vortex where only they could be. Their groans and sighs were the only sounds in the whirling world they made.

CHAPTER NINE

The days before the Winter Carnival seethed with reckless, frenetic activity that seemed to have no cohesive plan. Wyeth was sure the entire weekend would be a fiasco. She was assisting Solange in painting a huge mural that would be hung as the backdrop in the ballroom. Solange had confided to Wyeth that she had been working on the project for over two years. She had approached Colin with the idea of commemorating the history of Montbel on a canvas that could be used as a permanent hanging in the ballroom, and he had been enthusiastic. The past year he had been urging her to have it finished in time for the Winter Carnival.

"With just some of the background to finish, it looks like it will be done," Solange pronounced, a paintbrush poked into the kerchief round her head, pride in her voice. She and Wyeth both stepped back to admire the work. "I don't know what I'd done if you hadn't offered to help me, Wyeth. Thanks." Solange pressed her hand.

"Don't be silly. I've done nothing but fill in a little here and there. The artwork is yours, and it's beautiful. You should be very proud. Do you think the family will recognize themselves in the painting?"

"No," Solange answered, a smug smile on her face. "Look how long it took you to find Colin and yourself."

"Yes." Wyeth tried to fight the color she knew was staining her cheeks.

"Wyeth dear, are you embarrassed that I painted you and Colin in an embrace?" Solange teased.

"I'm not worried, but Colin might not like it."

"Colin might not like what, *ma belle*?" Colin had come up behind Wyeth and now encircled her waist with his arms, drawing her back against him. "Ahhhhh, you smell good even if you are covered with paint."

Wyeth turned to him at once, lifting her face to him to be kissed, which he did at once, ignoring the satisfied grin his sister gave him.

"Wyeth is worried about how you feel about the painting. See. This part." Solange pointed with a yardstick to a cloud sitting just behind the tower of Montbel.

Colin stared, a perplexed frown on his face. All at once a smile creased his face, and the arm holding Wyeth tightened. "Ah, Solange, you have painted us together. That's perfect, isn't it, *ma mie*?"

"See, Wyeth, I told you that Colin would like that," she crowed. "At first I had you alone on that cloud, brother mine. Then when I saw which way the wind was blowing, I had to add Wyeth's picture to yours."

Colin laughed and nodded, leaning over to kiss his smiling sister. Neither of them noticed the stricken look on Wyeth's face. "Now tell me, Solange, where have you put Émile and yourself?"

Solange's sweeping gesture picked up the two faces in the tower window of Montbel. "I can't believe this will be finished," Solange sighed. "I feel like Ulysses' wife, only I didn't tear up my work at night and begin again in the morning, but I sometimes felt like it." Her groan made Wyeth and Colin laugh.

"Mardi said that the sheers they are draping from the ceiling in the Arabian Room are finished in spite of Nate." Colin grinned, hugging Wyeth again.

In the laughing comments exchanged Wyeth was able to forget for a moment that she would be leaving Montbel in four days time. She had called Mr. Wingate and told him to apprise the housekeeper of her arrival. Wyeth only planned to stay in Boston a few days, then she would fly to California and stay with Monique until the baby was born. The two had talked two nights ago on the phone, and Wyeth's friend had been ecstatic at the thought of Wyeth coming to live with her.

"Wyeth, I can't believe it. The two of us again! What wild times we'll have. Come as quickly as you can."

"I will, Monique. Expect to see me in about a week and a half, barring complications."

Wyeth had rung off feeling that she had burned some of her bridges. She would tell Monique about the baby once she arrived in California.

More and more each day Colin showed his feelings for Wyeth in front of the family. He was making it plain to them and to anyone else that Wyeth was important to him.

Wyeth became more withdrawn and silent with the family as the time drew closer for her departure. Many times when she was with Nate and Annette she had to fight back tears. She caught both Mardi and Solange looking at her, their gaze questioning.

The day of the ball opening the Carnival Wyeth had not even decided on a dress. It would be a costume out of the history of Montbel, but Wyeth had been so distracted that she had not bothered to even think of anything.

She decided, as she stepped from the bath enfolded in a bath sheet, that she would just wear a gown. Standing before the full-length mirror, she dropped the towel and looked at herself. Yes, her tummy was rounding, and her breasts were larger, fuller. She smiled in secret happiness that she would have this child of Colin's to love when she wouldn't have him. He would be safe from her. Much as she tried to put the words of Amalie behind her, it had surfaced in her mind many times that perhaps she had been the cause of her parents' death and the death of Nate. If she was a jinx, then she would not allow Colin to be hurt by it.

She stopped short as she looked toward the bed and saw a

garment spread over the cover. The note on top told her that it had belonged to his grandmother, who had worn it to the Montbel Winter Carnivals. Colin had signed his name with love.

She lifted the cobwebby material of sea blue, a shade deeper than her eyes. It had an underdress of satin in an aquamarine shade.

Marie opened the outer door and came through, a smug look on her face. "Ah, madame, you have seen the dress. I have brought the jewelry that Monsieur Colin says will complete your ensemble, madame." Marie's lips pursed in irritation. "I hope you added all the herbs that you should to your bath, madame. Tcch, Monsieur Colin will be very angry that I do not attend you."

"Marie." Wyeth gave her a wan smile. "You wait on me hand and foot. You know that."

"Then, why do you look so pale, madame?" The sharp-eyed Quebecoise ran her eyes over Wyeth in a very Gallic, assessing way.

Wyeth lifted the gown from the bed, hoping to distract the watchful Marie. "Do you think this needs pressing, Marie?"

"Mais non, madame," Marie answered, shocked. "I, myself, have cared for it. Come, I will help you dress."

Wyeth managed to assure Marie that she could don her own clothes. But by the time she had adjusted the silk stockings she was to wear, Marie was in a tizzy to slip the sheer silk overdress on Wyeth's body.

"Voilà, madame. Enchanteresse." Marie clasped her hands when Wyeth finished affixing the sapphire drop earrings and the teardrop-shaped sapphire pendant.

Wyeth twirled in front of Marie, relishing the ohhs and ahhs of the delighted woman. She knew that the wispy material that clung to one shoulder and then draped in scarflike layers to just above the ankle was flattering to her tall, slim figure—that though she was covered from head to foot, the sheer material delineated her curves in a most provocative way.

The door leading to Colin's room opened, and he stood in the opening, his green eyes like lasers on her. At a wave of his hand Marie disappeared. "You're too beautiful to allow in public. I think I'll have to keep you up here."

Wyeth laughed, her breathing impeded. "What would you do with me? You look like you should be on the *Delta Queen* dealing cards, not trading words with me." Wyeth tried to laugh, but looking at him had made her mouth go dry. His black evening suit was accompanied by an oversize bow tie with a flowered silk vest with a pewter-colored background. He did look like a Mississippi riverboat gambler. Wyeth thought he was the most beautiful person in the world.

"To answer your question, love, as to what I would do with you," he purred. "First I would undress you, slowly, very slowly, then—"

"Colin, stop it." She put her hand to her cheek as though to mask the redness she knew would be there. "We'll be late."

His low laugh made her body temperature rise even more. "Here, love, I knew you would have no place to pin a flower." He handed her a tussie-mussie filled with white rosebuds that had a bluish tinge. The dangling ribbons were the same sea green as her dress.

"Colin, it's beautiful." Wyeth gulped, pressing close to him, needing his body warmth with a sudden desperation.

"Hey, what's this?" He took hold of her shoulders and held her back a fraction. "Are you feeling well?" His green eyes probed her face, snaking down over her body.

Wyeth stiffened, afraid that those all-seeing eyes could notice the rounding of her abdomen and guess its cause. "Not to worry." She tried to smile. "Émile says I'm tip-top."

"Yes." Colin spoke in a puzzled, slow way. "He said that you were in good shape."

"Well, then let's go." Wyeth held out her hand to him.

He caught it and pulled her close to him, his other hand closing over her breast. "Ummm, your body is filling out, *ma*

165

mie. I like it." He crooned this into her ear. He didn't see her swallow in nervousness. "Before we go, I must tell you that you are the most beautiful woman I have ever seen, and I'm happy you're mine." His kiss was gentle, reverent, tender.

Wyeth felt her throat clog with tears. She gripped her tussie-mussie and broke free of him. "Hurry," she uttered huskily.

The lobby was teeming with humanity in assorted dress. When a harlequin approached Wyeth and kissed her, she was startled until she recognized Kyle's laugh. He and Mardi were dressed as Pierrot and Pierrette. Solange and Émile were dressed as pirates.

"Solange, you look positively racy." Wyeth laughed.

"I agree," Émile grumbled. "I do not like so much of her to show . . . to others, that is." He leered at his wife, who leaned up to kiss his cheek.

Tante Cecile came toward them banging her stick on the floor, urging Solange and Mardi to hurry to the ballroom. The opening ceremony was about to begin.

Wyeth elected to walk with Tante since Colin had to accompany the other two women to help with the ceremony.

"We do not have to hurry, Wyeth. It will take time for them to begin. Shall we have some champagne?" Tante gave her an impish smile, looking far more regal dressed in her usual black than anyone present. "Ah, there is Amalie coming this way. *Dieu!* that dress, Amalie. What holds it up?" the old lady quizzed in dry tones.

Amalie's laugh did not reach her eyes when she greeted the old lady or Wyeth. "I am a gambling lady, to match Colin's outfit." She puffed on a long black cigarette holder.

"I think you look more like the Dragon Lady." Kyle looked Amalie up and down. "How fitting." He turned his head to the side and whispered to Wyeth.

She put her hand over her mouth to stifle the laugh.

Amalie's eyes trained on her like twin guns. "How sweet you

look, Wyeth. Imagine you getting into *Grand-mère*'s dress! You look like Camille."

"Really?" Wyeth bristled. "Well, unlike Camille, I feel quite strong—strong enough to take on anything." Wyeth's chin jutted forward.

Kyle guffawed, then at Amalie's glare and Tante's questioning look, he turned to signal one of the liveried waiters for more champagne.

More people began to move toward the ballroom. Wyeth was glad when Tante directed that they should follow along.

Even though there would be dancing in the lobby as well as in the ballroom, the opening ceremony was to take place in the ballroom.

They had no trouble maneuvering for a good spot when they arrived in the room decorated like a sultan's palace. The lobby had the look of a winter castle, with ice sculptures dotted here and there and giant firs propped against the pillars. Wyeth found the differing moods of the rooms pleasant.

"And do you like my idea of a sultan's room, Wyeth?" Amalie blew a stream of smoke through her nose, her cigarette holder acting as a pointer as she showed Wyeth the number of women in harem costume. "That's why I didn't dress that way. Colin's thought that we would look so well together is the other reason I dressed this way."

Wyeth stared at the other woman, willing the hot spear of jealousy to remain hidden.

Tante shushed them as Mardi and Solange, with a great deal of laughing, cut the ribbon and sounded the drum to let the festivities begin.

The music began and there was a great deal of milling about as some left for the lobby and some began dancing. With a great flourish Bill Balmain led Tante to the floor. As Wyeth watched them she saw Colin wending his way toward her, a smile on his face.

While she was still smiling at Colin she was whirled away in another pair of arms. She looked up, startled, into Luc's smiling face.

"I hope you wouldn't deny me the first dance, Wyeth?"

"You must know that I expected to dance this one with Colin." She looked at him in irritation.

"Don't be silly, Wyeth. Colin always has the first dance with Amalie. I'm sure they mean to marry this year," Luc crooned into her ear as he folded her closer.

"I don't believe you." She answered him through stiff lips, pushing against his shoulder to get room between them.

"Look for yourself." Luc shrugged.

Wyeth looked over her shoulder to see Amalie pressed against Colin as though she were glued to him. Colin's face was red. He was smiling down at Amalie, but Wyeth could sense that he was angry. She turned to look over Luc's black-clothed arm, staring blindly at the other dancers. Lord, if anyone had told her a year ago that she would actively want to see someone run over by a snowplow, she would have called them mad, she mused, finding the picture of Amalie in such a position most pleasant. *I'll get my sanity back when I leave Montbel,* she tried to soothe herself. She only managed to feel a wrenching pain at the thought.

She hardly heard Luc's words when he gave her over to Bill and assured her he would be back for another dance.

"Lovers' tiff?" Bill quizzed.

"What?" Wyeth answered, her mind in limbo.

"I asked if you and Colin quarreled. He's in one of the worst rages I've seen." Bill caught the quick look she gave him. "I mean it, Wyeth. I intend to stay out of his way. The way he's feeling now, he could dump me in the river and pack the ice down on me."

Wyeth smiled at him and shook her head. "Don't be ridiculous."

"I'm not. And you, lady, look as though you've lost your best friend. Do you want to tell me about it?"

"There's nothing to tell. Truly." Wyeth took a deep breath,

listening to Bill's banter. Soon it wasn't so much of an effort, and she began to laugh.

"That's better." Bill looked down at her, then lifted his head. "Uh, oh, here comes trouble. Hello, Colin. Have you come to steal Wyeth from me?"

Colin stared at his friend for some moments while Bill smiled at him. Then he looked down at Wyeth. "My dance, I think." He swept her into his arms, not looking at Bill again.

When Bill gave Wyeth a big wink behind Colin's back, she smiled.

Colin must have felt the change in her facial muscles against his and lifted his head to look at her. "What's so funny? The fact that you've danced with every man in the room but me?" he asked, his teeth grinding together. "Well, I'll tell you now, Wyeth, I'm not putting up with it."

Wyeth looked at him, her mouth agape. "I've danced with two men," she managed in failing accents.

"And neither of them me," he growled, making the couple dancing near them turn to stare. "What the hell do you think you're pulling?"

"Nothing," Wyeth breathed, watching the streaks of red high on his cheekbones, the rigid lines bracketing his mouth.

"Don't give me that," he whispered, the angle of his body menacing. "I saw you with Luc and Bill. What kind of game are you playing?"

Slack-jawed, Wyeth watched the green of his eyes turn a deep slate. He was in the grip of a consuming rage, and she couldn't reach for a word to assuage him. She felt her mouth work as she struggled to speak.

"If I have to manacle you to me I will, but you're going to learn to behave," he growled close to her ear.

"Me? Behave?" Wyeth felt her temper heat. "Don't you patronize me," she snapped, trying to pull back in his arms but not succeeding. "I'm not some naughty child you have to chastise, you arrogant—"

"Stop the name-calling, Wyeth." For some reason the anger seemed to dissipate in Colin as he looked down at her. "You have the shortest fuse of any woman I know," he mused, leaning down to press a kiss on her brow.

Wyeth's head snapped back. "And you're a chameleon! Do you know that?" she grated, watching that twist of a smile, wishing for an avalanche to bury him at that moment. "I do not have the least notion what you were roaring about before," she told him in measured tones, staring stonily at the bandleader.

"Bull, Wyeth. You know damn well what I mean, and unless you want to be the central attraction of a large scene right here, you'll pay attention to what I say."

"You are in need of psychiatric care." Wyeth spat the words into his flowered silk vest.

"If you're admitting that you drive me crazy, it's about time." Colin's lopsided grin made her stomach clench, her throat reacting as if she had swallowed alum.

"May I cut in?" Émile's easy smile ignored Colin's glare.

Wyeth pulled herself from his reluctant arms and turned to Solange's husband with a sigh of relief. She closed her eyes rather than see Colin's glowering face. "That man is impossible," she muttered to Émile who laughed.

"I must say it is a revelation to me to see the stalwart, unflappable brother-in-law laid low."

Wyeth leaned back and looked at Émile. "He doesn't even listen to reason. He just carries on."

"He's eaten up with jealousy, Wyeth. You know as well as I do, that's what the matter is. Put him out of his misery and marry him." Émile's eyes were stern.

"No." Wyeth's answer came through lips gone spastic.

"Have you told him about the baby?" Émile frowned at her.
"No."

"I thought not." He leaned down a bit and rubbed his chin on her hair. Émile was not much taller than Wyeth when she wore

170

high heels. "This is wrong. You must tell him. If you think it will take my Solange or Mardi long to guess your condition, then you are wrong. Would you like him to hear it from them that you're pregnant?"

"God, no." Wyeth swallowed a sob.

"Well, then, you must tell him. Why is it so hard for you, Wyeth? I know you love him."

Wyeth flinched. "Does it show so much?"

Émile shrugged. "My dear, to the Quebecois love is a very important thing. Perhaps not as important as their cows, but very close to it."

Wyeth gave a strangled laugh as Émile hugged her closer.

"Don't punish yourself so much, Wyeth. Tell Colin you love him and marry him."

"Émile, it's not that simple. I wish it were, but there's more . . ." Wyeth's voice trailed as she looked up and saw Colin's frozen face watching their every move. "Oh Lord, he certainly doesn't think I'm coming on with you, Émile!" she gasped as Émile turned to see where she was staring.

"He is a man, a very possessive man, Wyeth." Émile grimaced. "And he has a crippling left. I boxed only once in college and came to with Colin dribbling water on my face and telling me I was a sucker for a left. Wyeth, Solange will be put out with you if she becomes a widow, not to mention how I shall feel."

Wyeth laughed at the pained expression on his face. Her laugh faltered as she saw Colin stride their way.

Before he could reach them Solange was there, urging Wyeth to the powder room and telling her husband to make a run for the bar or hide behind Tante.

"My dear wife, do you question my courage?" Émile looked back at the stalking Colin. "On second thought, I'll hide behind Tante."

Wyeth was whisked into the powder room, where a giggling Mardi was waiting.

171

"Wyeth, I've never seen him that way. It's so funny. Mr. Cool, so very in charge of any situation, is ready to blow his top. Wyeth, what have you done to him?"

"Nothing. I've done nothing at all," she answered, giving Mardi a cross look, then glaring at a hooting Solange. She took her comb from the gold metal bag that hung from her shoulder by a long gold chain. Her hands were not quite steady. As she lifted her arms to comb she looked at the other images in the mirror behind her shoulder. They were looking at her body. Wyeth dropped her arms to her sides, her hands lifting in a protective gesture over her stomach.

"Wyeth, are you pregnant?" Solange breathed. "Damn that Émile, he said nothing." Solange accepted that it must be true without Wyeth's response.

Mardi gasped. "Of course, that's it. Is that why Colin's so upset tonight? I expected him to punch poor Mr. Armitage when he said hello to you this evening."

"Colin doesn't know." Wyeth swallowed as the other two squealed. "And you are not to tell him. I mean that. Promise me."

Mardi promised at once, but Solange tried to argue. Wyeth was adamant.

"I can't tell him, and I can't tell you why I can't tell him, but you must promise me." Wyeth's voice had risen.

The powder-room door opened, and one of the guests entered anxious to tell both Mardi and Solange how well the ball was going. It was some minutes before the three women were alone again.

"Wyeth, what's wrong? I know Colin would love children. Why won't you tell him?" Solange hissed as the door closed again.

Before Wyeth could say more Mardi put an arm around Wyeth's waist and squeezed. "We both promise, don't we, So-lange?"

172

Solange looked from one to the other. Her affirmative nod was reluctant.

The other three days of the Carnival were as hectic as the first, but Wyeth managed to keep herself busy with Mardi's children. She was ever aware that Colin was watching her, and she noticed that he would turn up at odd times, watching her with that brooding stare. Each time they made love Wyeth tried to savor the joy and not think of the agony their final parting would cause her. She was determined to leave on the last day of the festivities, figuring that her departure would be lost in the multiple guest departures at that time.

She had already written letters to the people who were most dear to her. The letter to Colin had taken hours. She told him that she had decided to live elsewhere and that she had deeded her shares of Montbel to him. She mentioned nothing about the baby or about the "jinx" that she had come to believe herself to be. She hadn't intended to tell him that she loved him, but the words seemed to write themselves across the bottom of the letter.

On the day she was to leave she deposited the letters into her own mailbox, knowing that Colin would look there when she left, trying to find out why.

She packed a minimum amount of clothing, knowing she could send for the rest or buy new things. Because of Nate's will, money would never be a problem.

Looking around her room, she sighed. She had been happier at Montbel than at any other place or in any other time in her life. She was leaving behind her true love. She gave a little smile as she looked at the hollow-eyed woman in the mirror. Oh, my, do you have memories!

She reached down to lift her overnight case just as the door crashed open. Mouth agape, she looked at Colin, his fists clenching and unclenching, his eyes a slate green and murderous.

"Just as I thought. Did you think I couldn't read those furtive looks Mardi and Solange were giving me? Whatever the hell you're trying to pull, it's over. And I do mean over. I've been patient with you, Wyeth, but that's over, too. I've arranged to have the damn banns posted. You're marrying me in three weeks."

CHAPTER TEN

Her wedding was beautiful, Wyeth thought hazily. Even Nate had been an angel. Her wish to have him as ring bearer was overruled by the entire family. Mardi told her firmly that she refused to allow Wyeth's wedding to be turned into a circus with Nate throwing the ring at Annette for some imagined slight. Mrs. Arbuthnot announced that she would be in charge of Nate for the day so that Mardi and Kyle would be able to concentrate on their duties as bride's matron and best man. Monique Almont had been ecstatic when Wyeth asked her to be maid of honor. Mr. Wingate had told Wyeth he would be most honored to give her away. Solange was going to be the other bride's matron, and Annette was to be flower girl. Wyeth had been adamant about that.

The gowns were made by a couturier in Montreal named Claude, who was a son of one of Tante's friends and considered to be the equal of his confreres in Paris.

Wyeth's dress was a waterfall of cream-colored handmade lace over a cream silk slip. The lace had been made and collected from Tante's friends and given to Claude to fashion the gown. It was off the shoulder, with long, tight sleeves ending in a point. The bodice was tight, requiring no bra, and the lace then fell from under her breasts in unpressed pleats to cascade behind her in a short train. It was regal, delicate, and very feminine. When Wyeth looked at herself, she gulped, feeling as teary as Marie, who sniffed all the while she dressed Wyeth. She wore the silk

175

veil belonging to Tante for a head covering and attached it to a coronet of cream roses. She carried Tante's prayer book covered in satin with cream rosebuds on the top. Colin gave her pinky cream pearls for her neck and ears.

From the time he had announced that they would marry, he had seemed to avoid her. The day that Émile had given them their blood tests, he had not said ten words to her.

Wyeth's anger at his high-handed ways kept her from telling him that she was pregnant. Neither all Solange's pleadings nor Émile's frowns changed her mind. She was damned if she would tell that bullheaded man anything.

The reception was held in the ballroom of Montbel, and the guests that were staying were invited, should they wish to attend. The chef had driven his staff with fanatic zeal, positive that no royal wedding could be as great as the one that he would personally oversee. There would be ice sculptures and three different types of wedding cake, the *pièce de résistance* being a tower of cheesecake in the shape of Montbel. When he had described this to Wyeth, she had told him not to do it, that it would be too much trouble. He had pinned her with his black-grape eyes and assured her that it would be done. She and Mardi had meekly backed away from the kitchen. There would be fountains of champagne and every canapé that an epicure might demand. Marie Clair would supervise the cake-decorating herself. Wyeth had the giddy feeling that she had been placed on a shelf to keep her out of the way. A bell would be rung to signal her part in the proceedings, someone to walk down the aisle of the old stone church, she was sure.

When she confided these fantasies to Solange and Mardi, they didn't laugh at her.

"We know just what you mean," Mardi answered her, her face contorted as she described Solange's wedding to Wyeth.

When the moment came to walk down the aisle on the arm of Mr. Wingate, she almost balked. Then she looked down the long stretch of stone carpeted with white linen and saw Colin watching her. She had not seen him enter from the vestry, had not seen him at all until he turned, with Kyle at his side, to face the back of the church where she would enter and follow Annette, Mardi, Solange, and Monique. Bill and Émile had led the procession. Now Colin's eyes compelled her forward. She had no power to disobey.

The words of the ancient church liturgy were a blur to her, but her hand had shaken when Colin slipped on the chased gold band that covered her finger almost to the knuckle. It had surprised her when he had insisted on wearing a matching band. She had had to struggle to fit the ring on his finger, feeling moisture bead her upper lip. Colin made no attempt to help her. Her responses were barely audible, his were deep and clear.

Before she could turn for the recessional Colin had taken hold of her arms and lifted her to him. The kiss he gave her was short, but hard and possessive.

Wyeth saw the melting looks that Monique and Solange gave her. Mardi was busy shushing Annette.

As they walked down the aisle Wyeth kept a smile fixed to her face, only relaxing when she came abreast of a stretching Nate, held in Mrs. Arbuthnot's arms.

His roars of "Y, Y, Y, Y," caused many smirks and much muffled laughter. Wyeth heard Colin's laugh and his muttered "little devil."

At the reception Wyeth accepted good wishes from a good share of people she neither knew nor whose names she could remember. Mrs. Almont held her and cried, saying over and over how happy she was that her dearest Wyeth was happy. Mr. Almont's eyes were red, and so were Mr. Wingate's. Monique sighed when Colin led Wyeth onto the floor to begin the dancing.

She felt his lips at her temple as he whirled her round the floor in a waltz. She leaned back to look at him, then looked away from the hot look in his eyes. He was angry with her still, but the anger did not mask the desire that he made no effort to hide.

"Now you are mine, *ma belle*. There will be no more running.

From now on, where you are, I will be; where I am, you will be."
He crooned, never losing a beat of the beautiful music.

"You make me sound like someone you've just purchased for your seraglio," Wyeth gasped, trying to keep on keel, both physically and mentally. She had had nothing to eat since rising and found that the annoying nausea she often noticed early in the morning had stayed with her.

"If that's the way you choose to look at it." Colin shrugged. Then his eyes ran over her in that assessing look he had. "You were so beautiful this morning. You're beautiful now. I guess that saying about all brides having a special glow is true."

So do all pregnant women, she mused to herself as the rocky feeling passed.

She danced with Mr. Wingate, with Kyle, with Émile. She relaxed and enjoyed the party.

When Luc led her to the floor, Colin glowered. Wyeth saw Mardi and Solange whispering to Monique, then the three of them laughing.

She danced with Bill, and Colin still glowered. Bill twinkled at her. "Your husband is a very jealous man, Mrs. MacLendon. I've known him most of my life and would never have said he would be this way with a woman." He shook his head. "Usually he just crooked a finger, and they came running. This time you're the one crooking the finger, and Colin's running."

Wyeth gaped at him. "That's just not true. I would never even attempt to tell that man what to do."

Bill threw back his head and laughed. A moment later Colin was beside them.

"My dance, I think," he grated, giving his best friend a black look.

Wyeth looked at Colin, her look as assessing as his had often been. Could he be as jealous as Bill seemed to think? Nonsense, Wyeth told herself, the thought pleasing her just the same. She pressed closer to him. She caught the quick, downward look he gave her, his eyes narrowed and piercing.

"It's time to go, Wyeth. We'll be staying at the house for a time. When the busy season slackens, we'll go to St. Thomas," Colin said, his tones flat, his eyes still roving her face, as though he wanted to see inside her. "You go and change. I'll meet you at the foot of the stairs. They'll expect you to throw your roses. I already told them I won't be removing your garter. There are too many men here watching you already. I'm damned if I'll let them stare at your legs." He ground the words through his teeth.

"I'll get ready, Colin," Wyeth said in a happy daze. Before she came to the top landing Amalie was there. "Darling, how long do you think Colin will last, after your lethal ministrations?" she cooed into Wyeth's ear.

"If you speak one word more, Amalie," Wyeth grated, her hands clenching, "I shall push you down this stairway, and I don't care who's around to see me do it."

White-faced, Amalie did a hundred-and-eighty-degree turn and descended the steps under her own power.

The words Amalie had whispered to Wyeth stayed with her even as Solange assured her that whatever she had said to Amalie must have been wonderful—that she hadn't seen her that put out in a long time.

Wyeth didn't understand why Solange and Monique insisted she wear the light silk suit in teal blue instead of the warm wool suit in the MacLendon tartan that she had planned to wear.

Mardi carried the full-length fur coat with the leather belt and matching hood as a triumphant offering. "Colin said I was to tell you that these rabbits were trapped for food, not for their skins, and that the coat is a gift from Albert and his cronies, who are true descendants of the voyageurs who roamed with the Indians almost three hundred years ago." Mardi took a breath and smiled at Wyeth.

Wyeth descended the stairs, Colin at her side, the three women behind them. Monique was crying when Wyeth urged her down the stairs to take her place with the other single women ready to catch the bouquet of roses.

179

With dead aim Wyeth threw the roses at Monique, then she and Colin ran through a shower of rice as they left the front door and sprinted for the horse-drawn sleigh that would take them to their home.

They hardly spoke as they wended their way through the snow-laden pines, the runners on the sleigh squeaking on the freshly fallen snow. Wyeth knew that years from then she would remember the warmth of Colin at her side, their breath clouding the air.

"Are you tired, Wyeth?" Colin inquired as he lifted her from the sleigh.

"No. I feel lazy, but I'm not tired." She answered him, trying to smile, trying to recapture the glow she had felt at the reception before she spoke to Amalie.

Colin explained that Marie Clair had had a crew working in the house: that was why there was a fire in the fireplace and the kitchen was stocked. "Marie Clair comes from the old school, where a man and a woman didn't surface for at least two weeks after the wedding." He laughed when Wyeth looked at him, open-mouthed.

They had dined on a very light repast, neither wanting too much food after feasting at the reception. Colin had placed a small tumbler of Montbel liqueur in her hand and then sat down close beside her on the overstuffed couch facing the fire. "Now are you going to tell me why you were leaving me?" Colin questioned her, looking down at the prismatic glass in his hand. Deep lines bracketed his mouth, his cheekbones pushing taut against his skin. "I'll tell you now, Wyeth, that nothing will make me set you free. You're mine under the law now, as you have been mine since the moment we met at Gaspard's. Nothing will change that—not now, not ever." He leaned forward, the glass hanging slackly between his knees, his eyes fixed on the flames.

"You knew even then?" Wyeth gave a shaky laugh.

"Yes." His head swung toward hers, pendulous and menacing.

180

"And I damn well keep what's mine. So if you don't want bloodied faces wherever we go, you tell that male coterie of yours what the score is."

"I don't have a coterie." Wyeth spoke in soft tones, her fingers itching to run through his chestnut hair, which stood in unruly waves from his restless hands.

"Then, what the hell do you call it?" He waved a hand at her as though to silence any reply. "No matter. You're mine now, Wyeth. You'll learn to love me, maybe never as much as I love you, but we'll be happy."

"You love me?" Wyeth's voice was choked.

Colin surged to his feet, tossing the liqueur down his throat in reckless disregard to the delicate liquid. "Come on, Wyeth, don't be coy. You know damn well I love you. I've shown it and told you in a hundred different ways. I want you, and I need you today and a thousand years from now." He threw the costly crystal into the fire. "I can please you when we make love. We have that. I'll make you happy. Now, tell me why you were running from me? Why were you going without telling me? I want the answer, Wyeth."

She looked at his solemn expression as he veered from looking down into the fire, his hands raised at his side, the fists clenched. She knew he would have his answer. She sighed and looked away from him. "It was what Amalie told me," she whispered through pasteboard lips.

"Amalie? What the hell has she got to do with us?"

"She loves you." Anger boiled in Wyeth.

"She loves what I could give her." Colin gave a shrug, dismissing the woman. "What could she say that would affect us?"

Wyeth gulped. "She said . . . that . . . I was an albatross, a jinx." Wyeth gazed at Colin's puzzled face and hurried on while she had the courage to tell him. "She said that I was the cause of my parents' deaths, that Nate wouldn't have died unless—" She squealed as Colin leaned over and lifted her from the couch.

"And you believed that damn twaddle? You, a law student,

181

who should have an analytical mind?" He lifted her high over his head, anger and amusement warring in his face. "You believed that crap? Let something like that come between us?"

Wyeth nodded, her feet dangling in the air.

"If I had known that, I'd have paddled you and packed Amalie off to Montreal. A good psychiatrist would make mincemeat of your reasoning, Wyeth, and the only reason I'm not paddling you now is because you've been ill and perhaps these aberrations occurred because of your illness. Either way, you listen to me now. Having you at my side is the only good luck I'll ever need. My life would be a desert without you, and nothing good would ever happen to me again if I didn't have you. If you don't believe me, look around Montbel and see the happiness you've brought with you. Look at little Nate and Annette, look at the self-confidence Mardi has evinced since meeting you. Kyle tells me they have never been happier. Solange considers you her dear friend. Even Émile—" Colin's brow darkened, and he clutched her closer. "I don't like the effect you have on other men. You will have to make up your mind that I'm enough for you, that having one male on a string is enough."

"You're not on a string." Wyeth giggled, feeling nine feet tall, yet utterly feminine.

"You're a femme fatale, *ma belle*," Colin growled, his mouth closing over hers, his breath mixing with hers. "I won't allow it."

"Take me to bed," she cooed against his mouth, feeling him stiffen. She watched his throat work with detached power.

"Tell me you want me, Wyeth." His voice was raw.

"No." She fastened her arms around his neck. "I'd much rather tell you something else."

"What?" His eyes ran over her face in restless heat.

"Take me to bed," she insisted, her fingers feathering his neck, loving the feeling when his body drew in on itself, like a bow-string about to release.

He swept her high into his arms, tremors running over his body as she pressed her lips to his cheek, his hair, his chin.

"You're mine, aren't you, Colin?" Possessive awe in her tone, she twined her hands through his hair.

"Yes, my own, I belong to you." Colin's voice was rough as he allowed her to stand next to their bed and began slowly devesting Wyeth of her things. One after the other, her newly purchased clothes were slung across the room like rags.

She felt the sudden tremor in his hands as he knelt in front of her to pull her panties down to her feet. She looked down at his head as he pressed his mouth against her stomach, "Colin, I want you, and I need you, but more than any of those I love you. I've loved you for ever so long, long before we made love the first time." She crooned the words in slow cadence to the top of his head.

His face snapped upward, the puzzled look wiped away, his eyes flaring in green fire, his facial muscles contorting in a blaze of feeling. He rose to his feet, his hands closing on her waist to whirl her in the air. "Say it again, *petite*. I need to hear it again," he growled, passion and laughter in his voice.

"Stop," Wyeth laughed, looking down at him. "You'll make me dizzy."

"Tell me," he demanded, his face alive and somehow relaxed.

"I love you," she muttered as she slid down his body. "If I live a thousand more years, it won't be long enough to tell you how much you mean to me."

"God, Wyeth." He pressed his mouth against the inside of her left wrist, his lips moving to her wedding ring, his eyes closed.

Wyeth fully meant to tell him about the baby at that moment, but Colin took her breath away. If she had been asked she would have said that Colin had taken her to every sensual peak there was, but Colin disproved it again for her. His mouth was everywhere on her body, igniting it, delighting in her in a way that was almost devastating.

When he pulled back to look at her, she reached for him, not wanting him away from her for a moment. His laugh turned to a snarl as her knowing hands began to fondle him in a feverish way. "Wyeth . . . my God, touch me, touch me."

Their climb to oneness was frantic but smooth, a gliding through white water to glad joining.

Wyeth yawned against Colin's chest and went to sleep, his chuckle and mutter, "But there's more, lady," the last sound she heard.

Colin woke her twice more in the night, making her body writhe in silken wonder, her hunger for him astonishing her.

Shafts of sunlight woke her, ungluing her heavy lids. She knew at once a rush of happiness, an awareness where she was. She knew at once that the heavy warmth around her body was Colin. In slow motion she turned her head to look at him. His lips were lightly parted, his face in repose like a boy's.

It made her breath come in gasps to think of having a tiny miniature Colin. She lifted one finger to outline his features in the air. She feared to waken him if she touched him. He was a very light sleeper. What if they had a girl? Wyeth mused. She would have lovely chestnut hair and deep green eyes. Or maybe blue eyes like her own. She would be a beauty, and Colin would hate all the boys who came to date her. Wyeth giggled, her one hand pressed to her mouth.

"And what are you laughing at, Mrs. MacLendon?" Colin mumbled, his lids lifting, a lazy smile on his lips. Before she could answer, Colin let out a prodigious yawn and growled, "I have never, but never, felt so good. I might run up one side of Montbel and down the other and carry you with me."

"I don't think that would be a good idea. I don't think my doctor would like it," Wyeth said, staring into his face.

He frowned, enfolding her closer. "But you're getting stronger every day and even a little chubby." He rubbed his hand in warm possession over her tummy. "And your breasts are much fuller, *ma belle*. Ummm, they're so lovely. By the summer you'll be telling me you want to diet. Don't bother asking. I won't let you." Colin nibbled her ear, his hand still rubbing in soft circles on her breast.

"By the summer I'll be a different shape altogether," Wyeth agreed, still watching him.

"I'll love you no matter what shape you are in," Colin said.

"Yes, I know you will, darling," she murmured, pressing his head to her. "But very soon you'll have to share me with . . . someone else."

His body contracted, then snapped taut, his mouth lifting from her body, his eyes green slate. "What the hell do you mean, Wyeth? Where do you—" His nostrils flared as though to release the steam inside him.

Wyeth put her fingers over his lips, smiling at him in a silky way. "My, you are a possessive man."

"Damn right."

"Darling, no need to fret yourself. That was just one of the things I wanted to tell you last night, but we were sidetracked." Wyeth placated, trying to pull his tense shoulders down to her again. "I wanted to tell you that I love you."

"That I like." Colin relented to nuzzle her shoulder.

"And the other was that you are going to be a father in about seven months," Wyeth soothed.

"How?" Colin croaked. "You can't be pregnant. The doctors said that you couldn't." He spoke huskily, stroking her, his hand going to her rounded abdomen, to touch and pet; then he looked at her questioningly.

"The usual way is how we did it," Wyeth smirked. "And the doctors said that I *might* not be able to conceive. Of course, they didn't know I would run into such a virile man."

Colin put his head on her breasts. "And you would have run from me? You would have been alone. My God, I'll kill Amalie if I see her again."

"Don't say that," Wyeth sighed, her arms enfolding him. "Tell me you don't mind," she whispered.

He lifted his head, his eyes moist. "Wyeth, is it safe for you? Will you be all right? No baby is worth you, my love."

"Étienne Aubert is a very good obstetrician. Émile says so."

"He knew?" Colin frowned at her, then his eyes narrowed in thought. "And Mardi and Solange knew. I thought they looked at me in a funny way." He looked at Wyeth in a proprietary way. "This is mine. I should have been the first to know."

"Darling, I didn't tell them. They guessed, and Émile found out when he examined me at your orders," Wyeth soothed.

"If I weren't so happy, I'd ring a peal over my whole family," Colin muttered. He lifted his head in horror. "I made love to you last night. Was that all right?"

"Of course, silly. Dr. Aubert was quick to assure me on that score."

"He'd better be damned professional with you if he wants to live long." Colin frowned down at her unclothed body. "I don't like the thought of him seeing you like this."

Wyeth arched her body in wanton invitation. "No one ever sees me like this but you, darling."

Wyeth heard the ragged sound of his indrawn breath before his body covered hers.

LOOK FOR NEXT MONTH'S
CANDLELIGHT ECSTASY ROMANCES™

When You Want A Little More Than Romance—

Try A Candlelight Ecstasy!